W9-AXE-482

Absolutely Normal Chaos

EAST NORTHPORT PUBLIC LIBRARY
EAST NORTHPORT, NEW YORK

Also by

SHARON CREECH

Walk Two Moons

Pleasing the Ghost

Chasing Redbird

Bloomability

The Wanderer

Fishing in the Air

Love That Dog

A Fine, Fine School

Ruby Holler

Granny Torrelli Makes Soup

Heartbeat

Who's That Baby?

Replay

The Castle Corona

Hate That Cat

The Unfinished Angel

SHARON CREECH

Absolutely Normal Chaos

HARPER
An Imprint of HarperCollins*Publishers*

With warm thanks to Marion Lloyd

Absolutely Normal Chaos
Copyright © 1990 by Sharon Creech
First published in Great Britain in 1990 by Macmillan Children's Books
All rights reserved. Printed in the United States of America. No part of this book may be used or reproduced in any manner whatsoever without written permission except in the case of brief quotations embodied in critical articles and reviews. For information address HarperCollins Children's Books, a division of HarperCollins Publishers, 195 Broadway, New York, NY 10007.
www.harpercollinschildrens.com

Library of Congress Cataloging-in-Publication Data
Creech, Sharon.
Absolutely normal chaos / Sharon Creech
p. cm.
Summary: Thirteen-year-old Mary Lou keeps a summer journal which chronicles her first experiences with romance, homesickness, and death.
ISBN 978-0-06-440632-1
[1. Homesickness—Fiction. 2. Death—Fiction. 3. Cousins—Fiction. 4. Fathers and sons—Fiction. 5. Families—Fiction.] I. Title.
PZ7.C8615Ab 1996 95-22448
[Fic]—dc20 CIP
AC

Typography by Michelle Gengaro-Kokmen

16 OPM 47

Revised paperback edition, 2012

For Karin and Rob Leuthy
and all our Creeches

Dear Mr. Birkway,

Here it is: my summer journal. As you can see, I got a little carried away.

The problem is this, though. I don't want you to read it.

I really mean it. I just wanted you to know I did it. I didn't want you to think I was one of those kids who says, "Oh yeah, I did it, but I lost it/my dog ate it/my little brother dropped it in the toilet."

But please PLEEEASSSE DON'T READ IT! How was I to know all this stuff was going to happen this summer? How was I to know Carl Ray would come to town and turn everything into an odyssey? And how was I to know about Alex . . . ? Sigh.

PLEASE DON'T READ IT. I mean it.

Sincerely,
Mary Lou Finney

Tuesday, June 12

I wish someone would tell me exactly what a journal *is.* When I asked my mother, she said, "Well, it's like a diary only different." *That* helps. She was going to explain more, but Mrs. Furtz (the lady who just moved in across the street) called to say that my brother Dennis was throwing eggs at her house, and my mother went berserk so she didn't finish telling me. How am I supposed to write a journal if I don't even know what one is?

I wouldn't be doing this anyway, except that Mrs. Zollar asked me to. She's an English teacher. She asked us to keep a journal this summer and bring it in (in September) to our new English teacher.

So, new English teacher, I guess I better say who I am. My name is Mary Lou Finney. I live at 4059 Buxton

Road in Easton, Ohio. I have a normally strange family. Here's our cast of characters, so to speak:

Sam Finney (whose age I am not allowed to tell you) is the father. He is a pretty regular father. Sometimes he likes us and sometimes we drive him crazy. When we are driving him crazy, he usually goes out in the garden and pulls some weeds. When he is at work, he is a geologist and spends his days drawing maps.

Sally Finney (whose age I am also not allowed to tell you or anyone else) is the mother. She also is a pretty regular mother. Sometimes she drools all over us and sometimes she asks my father if there isn't something he can do about us. When we are driving *her* crazy, she usually cries a little. When she is at work, she is an oral historian and spends her days tape-recording stories that elderly people tell her. I think that by the time she gets home to us, she is a little tired of hearing people talk.

Maggie Finney (seventeen years old) is the oldest daughter. She's my sister. She is your basic boy-crazy, fingernail-painting, mopey ole sister with whom I have the misfortune of sharing a room. She does not like me to touch her things.

Mary Lou Finney (thirteen years old) is the next oldest. That's me. I don't know what I am. I am waiting to find out.

Dennis Finney (twelve years old) is the kind of brother

who will climb a tree with you one minute and tell on you the next. He gets into a fair amount of trouble (such as getting caught throwing eggs at Mrs. Furtz's house, breaking windows with apples, etc.), but he is okay other than that.

Doug Finney (better known as Dougie) (eight years old) gets lost in the middle of everyone else. He's skinny as anything and follows everybody else around. He's quiet and more serious than the rest of us, so nobody minds him tagging along, but he calls himself the "poor little slob."

Tommy Finney (four years old) is the spoiled-baby type kid. We think he's cute as anything, and so he gets away with murder. He's the messiest eater you've ever seen.

This journal is not as hard as I thought. I just hope I am doing it right. It would be terrible to do it all summer and then take it in and have someone look at it and say, "Oh, but this isn't a journal, dear."

I tried to ask Mrs. Zollar a million questions about the journal when she gave it to us, but Alex Cheevey said, "Geez. We don't want to know *too* much about it. Then we'll have to do it *right.* Can't you ever keep quiet?"

And now I will reflect on that. I used to think Alex Cheevey was cute, because his skin is always a little pink, like he's just been running a race, and his hair is always clean and shiny, and once we had to do an oral report together and even though I did most of the work, he patted me on the back when we were done, as if he realized what a good job I did, and he is certainly the best player on the basketball team and so graceful when he runs and dribbles the ball. But now, as I reflect on it, I see he is really a jerk.

Wednesday, June 13

I've been sitting here thinking about last Friday, the last day of school, when I heard Christy and Megan talking about Christy's party. I wasn't invited. They are always having these parties, but they only invited me once, and that was because I took Megan some books when she was sick and spent three hours explaining the homework and even doing some of it for her, and so for about a week she was my friend.

But the party was the stupidest (I know there is no such word as stupidest) thing I have ever seen, with the girls all giggling in the middle of the room, and the boys all leaning against the walls, and then they put on the records and started dancing, just the girls with the girls, until finally a slow song came on and some of the boys danced slow with some of the girls just to hang all over their necks, but no one asked me to dance, so I had to stand by the food and pretend to be hungry as anything.

I keep forgetting to reflect on things. I will reflect on these parties. If I was a boy, I would wish they would plan something interesting, like maybe a game of basketball.

After our last exam, Christy came slinking up to Alex and said, "Welllll, Alex, see you tonight." (I am going to try some dialogue here.)

Alex looked down at his shoes and said, "Unnnh."

Christy wiggled her shoulders and said in this thin little voice, "Well, you *are* coming, *aren't* you?"

Alex put the toes of his shoes together like he was pigeon-toed and said, "Unnnh."

Christy pushed her face right up next to his and said, "It's at eight o'clock. Don't forget!" Then she patted her hand on his shoulder a few times and turned around and wiggled away. Lord.

I walked home from school with Beth Ann. Beth Ann Bartels is my best friend, I guess. We're very different, but we have been friends, with no fights, since the fourth grade. I tell her just about everything, and she tells me *everything,* even things I do not want to know, like what she ate for breakfast and what her father wears to bed and how much her new sweater cost. Sometimes things like that are not interesting.

But, anyway, on the way home, as Beth Ann and I

were passing the Tast-ee Freeze, it suddenly occurred to me that school was over and it was summer and I was going to have to start having fun the very next day and I wouldn't see most of the people at school for three months. Beth Ann and I live on the farthest edge of the school district, at least two miles from school. Everyone else seems to live on the other side of the school. Well, it was a little sad to realize that school was over. Then I thought, boy, isn't that just typical? You wait and wait and wait for something, and then when it happens, you feel sad.

I always stop at Beth Ann's house before I go on home. We have this little routine. We go in and the house is quiet, not at all like my house, which is a complete zoo at any hour of the day or night. Her house is always immaculately clean, as if someone had just raced through with a duster and a vacuum cleaner or as if no one really lived there. Our house always has people's clothes lying all over: socks on the stereo, jackets on the kitchen table, everyone's papers and books clumped in piles on chairs and counters. So I like to stop at Beth Ann's house before I go home.

Beth Ann's parents both work and so does her older sister Judy, so we have the house to ourselves. We always go into the kitchen, and I sit at the table while Beth Ann takes out a bottle of Coke and a bag of potato chips. It amazes me that there is always Coke and potato chips. In our house stuff like that would disappear in about ten minutes.

On the way home from Beth Ann's, I ran into Alex Cheevey, who doesn't live anywhere near here. He had his hands in his pockets and he looked very pink. When he got up close to me, I said, "Alex Cheevey? What in the world are you doing over here?"

He said, "Oh. Do you live over here?"

I said yes, I did.

He said, "Oh. What a coincidence."

I said, "Why?"

He said, "Oh. Well, I know someone over here."

I said, "On Buxton Road?" I was a little surprised, because Buxton Road is a very short road and I know everyone on it and I had never seen Alex Cheevey here before.

He said, "Oh. No."

I said, "On Winston?" Winston is the next street over.

He said, "Oh. Yeah."

I said, "Who?"

I am getting tired of writing "I said" and "he said." Sometimes you don't have to put those words just to know who is talking, so I'm not going to.

"Oh. The Murphys." (That's Alex talking.)

"The Murphys?" I'd never heard of the Murphys.

Well, anyway, we talked on like that for a while and he asked me if I was going to Christy's party. I told him that no, I was not going, and I was glad I wasn't going.

So that was on the last day of school, and when I got ready to go to bed and thought about everyone being at that party, including Alex, I sort of wished I was there too. Not that I thought it would be any fun, but because I didn't have anything much to do that night. I'm not used to this idea of vacation yet.

Boy, if I write this much every day of the vacation, I will need ten journals. Wouldn't Mrs. Z. be amazed???

For your sake, though, mystery reader, I hope things get a little more interesting. God.

Thursday, June 14

Well, I have to admit that we did get an *interesting* bit of news today! I almost missed it entirely, because of all the commotion at the dinner table. There is always commotion at the dinner table—you can hardly hear yourself eat. We had spaghetti, and Dougie doesn't like spaghetti and was pushing it around his plate and slopping sauce all over, and so Dennis punched him and Dougie started crying and Mom told him to be quiet and eat his spaghetti because he wasn't getting anything else. And

Dougie said, "I'm just a poor little slob," and Dennis said, "That's right."

In the middle of all that Dad said, "Had a letter from Radene today." Radene is married to Dad's brother, Uncle Carl Joe, and they live in West Virginia. "Did you see it?" Dad said. (He meant the letter.)

"No, I didn't see it. Dougie, if you don't stop that hollering right this minute—" (Just to give you an idea of how hard it is to follow the conversation.)

"Well, she wants to know—"

"Dennis, are you aggravating the situation? If you are—" Mom can hardly eat, she's so busy trying to figure out who's causing the trouble. All this time Tommy is throwing spaghetti all over the floor and it's in his hair, but that's just the way he eats.

"Sally, are you listening or not?" My dad is getting annoyed because he can't stand all this commotion, and it happens every night.

"Why, of course I'm listening, Sam. Dennis, put your hands on the table where I can see them."

"Radene wants to send Carl Ray up here." Dad eats a meatball.

About this time Dougie is so upset that he spills his milk right onto my plate.

"Sam, can't you *do* something about them?" Mom said.

My dad looked up from his meatballs and spaghetti and said, "Somehow, I don't think that any of my study of rock formations and fossils prepared me for this."

I don't know how we all settled down, but we did for a time, and that's when Mom finally realized what Dad had said about ten minutes earlier.

"Radene said *what*?"

"She wants to send Carl Ray up here."

Carl Ray is one of Aunt Radene's and Uncle Carl Joe's seven children. He's my cousin.

"What do you mean, she wants to send Carl Ray up here?" My mom didn't look too happy about this.

"Just temporarily," my dad said. "He wants to get a job. No work down there. It'll just be for a little while, until he gets a job and gets on his feet."

"Send him *here*? To *this* house? To live with *us*?" As I said, my mom didn't seem too happy about all this.

Then she said, "Don't you think that's a little strange, Sam? There are lots of other places he could go, aren't there?"

My father shrugged. Sometimes he doesn't like to elaborate.

"And just where exactly will we put him?" My mother had stopped eating by now.

"Well, we could put the boys in together—"

"All three of them?"

"Wouldn't hurt 'em. Then we could put Carl Ray in the little room where Tommy is now."

"In the *nursery*? Sam, are you *serious*?"

"It's just temporary. A month. Maybe two months. Maybe the summer—"

"The *summer*? Are you serious?" My father was closely examining his meatball. My mom kept going. "And *when* does she want Carl Ray to come up here?"

My father was chewing when he answered. "Saturday."

Mom almost choked. "*Saturday? Saturday?* Sam, today is *Thursday*! You can't be serious. Why didn't she phone?"

"They don't *have* a phone. You know that," he said.

Maggie said, "How primitive!" Maggie could not exist for one single day without a phone, I can assure you.

So Carl Ray comes the day after tomorrow. That should be interesting. I have to admit I'm sort of surprised, mainly because the West Virginia Finneys hardly ever leave West Virginia. The only time I ever have heard of Uncle Carl Joe venturing this far north was when he visited my father and met Aunt Radene, a long time ago.

My parents talk about that time whenever New Year's Eve rolls around. That's because they had one heck of a New Year's Eve, and Uncle Carl Joe and Aunt Radene fell in love "at first sight." Anyway, Uncle Carl Joe whisked Aunt Radene off to West Virginia (I think they got married first), and I bet they haven't left West Virginia since. They never visit *us* anyway. They have too many kids to fit in the car. We've been to their house, though.

I can hardly remember which cousin Carl Ray is, but Maggie told me later that he is the one with the white-blond hair and he is seventeen years old, the same age as Maggie. This should be *real* interesting.

Friday, June 15

Lord, what a day. This business about Carl Ray is getting out of hand. When I got up this morning, I noticed that instead of my mom's usual individual notes for each of us, there was just one note by the telephone that said: "Magggggie or Mary Louuuuuu, call me at work when you get up. Love, your old Mommmmmmmm."

Right away, I knew that if she didn't leave a list for each of us, it wasn't because there was nothing for us to do. I know Mom better than that. It probably meant that there was so much to do, she couldn't write it all down. And I was right.

She gave me a list of things a mile long, and all because of Carl Ray. Mainly we had to move everything out of Tommy's room into Dennis and Doug's room, and bring the spare bed down out of the attic and put it in

Tommy's room, and wash windows, and on and on.

Actually, it was all kind of fun for a while. We like to move things around. But when Dennis and I were bringing down the bed from the attic, we had a slight problem.

The springs for the bed are these old metal heavy ones, and we were having trouble getting them down the stairs of the attic, so we decided to slide them down. I was at the top and Dennis at the bottom, when all of a sudden the springs lunged forward and crashed into the door at the bottom, putting a huge crack in it, and then they fell forward on Dennis, and a piece of spring tore right into his knee and he started howling and the blood was pouring all over.

It was a mess. Maggie was yelling at Dennis to stop screaming and Dennis was screaming at me saying it was my fault and I was screaming at Dennis saying it was not and Dougie was screaming because he hates blood and Tommy was screaming because everyone else was screaming.

Then Maggie ran over to Mrs. Furtz's, who was the only neighbor home. I'm sure she wasn't exactly thrilled about helping us after Dennis smashed eggs on her house, but she came running over in her curlers and bathrobe and told me to wrap up Dennis's leg while she changed her clothes, and then she would take him to the emergency room. So I put a pillowcase around his leg, trying to remember my first-aid class. I wanted to try a tourniquet, but Dennis wasn't having any part of it. He just kept saying he was going to throw up. I hate it when people throw up.

Maggie called Mom, who said she would meet Mrs. Furtz and Dennis at the emergency room. I wanted to go too, but Maggie said that Mom said that *she* should go and I should stay here with Tommy. I think Maggie made that up.

Maggie and Dennis were gone forever. I thought Dennis died or something. Well, that does happen sometimes. We read a Robert Frost poem called "Out, Out—" in English class last year about a boy who got his hand cut near off from a buzz saw and he died while his hand was being sewn back on. That was this saddest poem, because at the end of it no one seemed to care about this boy dying. They just went on with their business.

I have to admit that even though I really like Dennis and would miss him a lot if he died, I kept thinking maybe I would get his new bike. But then I felt so guilty for thinking that, I dragged the mattress down out of the attic by myself and got the whole bed together with only a little help from Dougie, and then I made up the bed and took down the curtains and put them in the wash and cleaned the windows and had just about everything done when Maggie and Dennis strolled in with Mom, who had taken the rest of the day off from work.

Mom hardly even noticed all the work I had done, she was so busy drooling all over Dennis. Dennis was being pathetic. He wasn't even near dead—just had this huge bandage on his knee. He spent the entire day lying on the couch in the living room, moaning. He got ice cream and ginger ale, and Mom kept going in and feeling his forehead (his *forehead*! It was his knee that got hurt!).

Mom only said two things about Carl Ray's room. First she said, "Thank you, girls, for setting that up."

Girls! And Maggie just smiled and said, "It was nothing." Ha.

And the only other thing Mom said was, "I can't imagine Carl Ray in the *nursery*!"

It does seem a little funny. The room has yellow walls (that's not so bad) and frilly white curtains with yellow bunnies on them (now that's bad), and a little border around the top of the walls that also has yellow bunnies on it.

I keep wondering what it will be like with Carl Ray here. Whenever I ask Maggie to tell me more about him, though, she acts like it's no big deal. But I did notice that she put a bottle of her perfume in the bathroom, which is strange because usually she hides it in her drawer so I won't touch it.

Everybody seems so excited about Carl Ray coming. Even Mom, which surprises me, because I thought she didn't want him to come. I keep wondering how we're all going to manage getting in and out of the bathroom. That will make eight of us who have to share it. With seven of us now, there's already a problem. There is another one downstairs, but it only has a toilet and a sink.

Mom told me and Maggie that we have to wear our bathrobes now. I wonder if Carl Ray will wear a bathrobe.

Saturday, June 16

Well. Carl Ray has arrived.

It's almost midnight and Maggie is out with her boyfriend, Kenny, and boy, is Dad mad. She hasn't even *seen* Carl Ray. That's not why Dad is mad: He's mad because Maggie and Kenny left at noon and they were going to the beach and they didn't say what time they'd be back. She's in real trouble, I think. Everyone else went to bed, but Dad is downstairs waiting.

Well, about Carl Ray. What a disappointment *he* is. I was expecting something quite, quite different. We waited around all morning looking out the windows. Around noon Dad came back from Alesci's. He does the grocery shopping on Saturdays, and afterward he stops at Alesci's, which is an Italian deli, and he buys a bunch of ham and two loaves of hotttttt, freshhhhhh bread, and as soon as he gets home and we put away the groceries, we always dive into the hot bread and ham and make these enormous sandwiches. It's the best part of Saturdays, usually.

Just as we finished putting the groceries away and seconds before we were going to start cutting up that great bread, Dougie comes into the kitchen yelling, "Carl Ray! Carl Ray! There's a guy at the door who says he's Carl Ray!" What timing.

Carl Ray is tall and skinny, about as skinny as a person can be and still be alive. He has the blondest hair, almost white, and it sticks out in places like at the top of his head and by his ears where it is cut kind of short. He is real pale and has a million freckles all over his face and his arms, which were the only parts of him sticking out, but I bet he has those freckles everywhere. He has tiny little eyes and a tiny nose; in fact, his whole head looks like a miniature of a real person's head. So there is this tiny little head perched on top of this tall, thinnnnnn body, and off this body hang two longgggg, thin, freckled arms, and two longgggg, thin legs, and two long, thin hands and two longgggg, thin feet. What a guy.

Carl Ray has hardly talked at all yet, and Mom thinks it is because he is nervous. He keeps looking down at your feet and never looks into your face.

After we got him out of the living room and into the kitchen, Mom told us kids to wait and not hog the ham and bread until Carl Ray had a chance to get his. I can see it all now: Carl Ray is going to take over. He's the only one with his own room and he's the only one who ever got to grab six slices of ham and four slices of bread before anyone else could even touch it.

After lunch, Mom showed Carl Ray to his room and drooled all over, apologizing for the bunnies and stuff. He didn't say one word, just looked around and put his suitcase down. Mom said he might like to rest awhile (probably because he ate such a HUGE lunch), and he nodded and closed his door. Then Mom told us all to be quiet until he got up. Brother.

So all afternoon everybody tiptoed around, but he didn't even come out of his room until he smelled dinner cooking. Just as we put everything on the table, he appeared. He kind of sneaks up on you.

Mom told Carl Ray to sit at the end of the table, opposite Dad. That's a "special" seat that we all take turns sitting in. I don't know why it is special; it just is.

For being a skinny person, he sure eats a lot. He had four pieces of chicken, three helpings of mashed potatoes, about a ton of green beans, three glasses of milk, and two helpings of cake. Mom kept looking at the chicken, as if she could make more pieces appear by staring hard enough. And when Dennis went to take his second piece, she gave him a dirty look, and said, "Wait a bit; we have com-pa-ny."

After dinner, we all sat around watching TV. Carl Ray sat in my dad's favorite chair, the one none of us is ever allowed to sit in when Dad is in the room. During the whole night, Carl Ray never said one single word, even though sometimes Mom or Dad would say something to him. He just nods or shakes his head; sometimes he grunts a little.

When everybody started going to bed, Mom said, "Now let Carl Ray get in the bathroom first," so we all waited around while he went into his room and shut his door. We waited and waited and waited. Finally, Dougie went over and peeked under the door and whispered that the light was out! Doesn't Carl Ray even wash up or brush his teeth before he goes to bed?

It's one o'clock and Maggie isn't home. I bet Dad is still waiting in the living room. I sure wouldn't want to be her tonight.

Sunday, June 17

Carl Ray is going to drive me cra-zeeee. And so is Maggie. Lord.

First, Maggie. She got home at two a.m. I know, because she came into the room crying and throwing her shoes around and she turned the light on, and needless to say, I wasn't sleeping through that. When I asked her what was wrong, she said, "Ohhh! Everything."

I said, "Like what?"

"Everything. Kenny. Dad. Ohhhh. I'm so mad."

She was mad? "Why are *you* mad?"

She glared at me. "Because I told Kenny we had to call and he kept saying, 'Yeah, yeah,' and because Dad never lets me have any fun, and because now he says I'm grounded for at least two weeks and next Saturday is only the biggest party I'll ever be invited to, and because Dad told Kenny not to show his face around here until he could be a gentleman, and because Kenny probably will never speak to me again."

Then she threw herself down on her bed and started pounding her pillow and sobbing. I hate it when she does that. It looks like a movie. I told her Carl Ray had arrived.

"So what?" she said.

"Don't you want to hear about him?"

"No!" She was pounding the pillow again. This morning she stayed in bed until noon, and then she was in the bathroom for about two hours, and when she came downstairs finally, her eyes were all puffy and she wasn't talking to *anybody*.

Whenever Dad came into the room, she would go storming out. Finally, Dad told her if she didn't quit her "theatrics," he was going to ground her for a month, for starters. That made her shape up a little. She's still pretty mopey, and every time the phone rings she jumps for it, but at least she's talking to people a little bit.

For instance, she's the only one who seems to be able to talk to Carl Ray and get some words out of him. I heard her asking him some questions and he actually answered her with words. It went something like this:

"So I hear you're going to look for a job? Is that right, Carl Ray?"

"Yup."

"When?"

"Tomorrow."

"Where are you going to look?"

Long pause by Carl Ray. Then, "Don't rightly know."

"What sort of work are you interested in?"

Long pause by Carl Ray. "Don't rightly know."

"What are you good at?" That's Maggie all right. She

just keeps picking away and picking away like a vulture or something.

I was glad that I didn't have to try to make conversation with him. It's painful. Besides, I was already mad at him for spoiling my day. I was supposed to go over to Beth Ann's at eleven and we were going to go and hang around the pool, but Mom said I had to wait until Carl Ray got up so I could make up his bed and stuff. I said, "What? Why do I have to make up his bed?"

"Because you're responsible for the upstairs and you know you can't leave until it's clean."

"But why can't he make up his own bed, like everyone else?"

We have this hugely complicated chore system at our house. Every year we have a big meeting where we're supposed to swap jobs. It begins all nice and civilized, but ends in a shouting match: "Dennis always gets the easy jobs!"—"I do not!"—"I'll trade you vacuuming for dusting!"—"No way!"—"That's not fair!" You get the picture?

We're all supposed to make our own beds, but my main chore is to vacuum and dust the upstairs. I had to clean the bathrooms last year (eck!), but Dennis has that wonderful job now.

Back to Carl Ray. I said, again, "Why can't Carl Ray at least make up his own bed, like everyone else?"

"Because Carl Ray is our guest, Mary Lou."

That drove me crazy. Whenever I'm going to spend the night at someone's house, my mom tells me that I must be very considerate and always make my bed up neatly as soon as I get up. When I reminded her of this, she said, "Well, his mother might not have told him that. If he's still here in two weeks, he'll make his own bed."

"But if I don't go now, Beth Ann might not wait—"

"Now don't you argue with me. If you're going to argue, then you can stay home all day."

Boy, are people touchy lately. So I waited and waited. I even tried making noise upstairs, like turning on my radio.

Mom said, "Turn that off! You might wake Carl Ray." *(Exactly.)*

I waited a little longer and decided to go ahead and do the vacuuming in the other bedrooms and the hallway, so all I would have left to do would be Carl Ray's room.

Mom came flying up the stairs after me and flipped off the switch and said, "I *told* you to keep quiet up here!"

"But—"

"Mary Lou Finney!" When Mom says "Mary Lou Finney," she means business.

I kept calling Beth Ann, about every fifteen minutes, telling her Carl Ray still was not up and I couldn't leave until I did maid service for him. Finally, at twelve thirty, Beth Ann said, "It doesn't sound like you're ever going to get out of there. I'm going for a ride with my parents."

Boy, was I mad. When ole Carl Ray finally did stroll out of his room about one o'clock, I nearly pushed him over when I passed him. Sure enough, he didn't make his bed, so I did, and I picked up all his stupid gum wrappers that he left all over the floor and I vacuumed his stupid room. I was done by one fifteen, but then I had nowhere to go.

All Carl Ray did the whole entire day was sit in front of the television set chewing gum and watching whatever happened to come on. I don't think he even got up to change the channel. A real live wire, this Carl Ray.

What a boring day, with everyone just wandering in and out of rooms: Maggie avoiding Dad, Dad avoiding Maggie, me avoiding Carl Ray, all of us avoiding Mom, who was doing the laundry and if you get in her way, she makes you fold clothes or iron.

I was so bored, I even went with Dennis and Doug over to the field behind Mrs. Furtz's house.

There's a big old tree there that sits in a little dip in the ground and its branches hang real low, so if you crawl into the dip and under the branches, it's like a fort inside. Anyway, we went in and cleaned out some leaves and junk, and we moved the rocks that cover a hole we dug last year. It was funny to see what we put inside: a box of matches, a newspaper, a red ball, two packs of chewing gum, a treasure map we had drawn (the treasure consists of fifty cents, which we buried in another hole about a hundred yards away), and a deck of cards. Real exciting.

We hung around there awhile, climbing the tree (I have to admit that even though I am thirteen years old, I still love to climb trees), pretending we were looking out for enemies, and playing cards. We should have brought some food. We were going to chew the gum, but it was all gross from being in the ground for a whole year.

It's funny, but thinking about the fort and the field now reminds me of something that happened there about four years ago. It's a stupid thing, but I'll write it down anyway. I can always rip it out later if it's too embarrassing.

I guess I was nine years old then, and there was this boy named Johnny White who lived down the street from us. He was Dennis's friend really, and he was a year younger than I was. Anyway, one day Dennis, Johnny, and I were over in the forest running around the trees and singing some stupid song. Then Dennis said he was going home to get us some sandwiches so we could have a picnic. Johnny and I walked all around the field with the tall grass where there were bunches of buttercups too, and I picked one and rubbed it under Johnny's chin, which made him laugh because he had never seen anyone do that before. And all of a sudden, I don't know what came over me, but I just reached over and kissed Johnny White on the lips! I don't think I had ever kissed anyone but my parents on the lips before. And I was real surprised because his lips were so soft, but they didn't taste like anything at all. So I kissed him again, mainly just to see if I could taste anything.

We didn't even hear Dennis coming. The first I knew he was there was when he said, "Hey, what're you doing?"

But then we all just ate our sandwiches and went back to messing around in the forest, climbing trees, and stuff, and I didn't think any more about kissing Johnny until the next day.

What a *mess*. Mrs. White called my mother. My mom said Mrs. White was almost hysterical. Mrs. White said that Johnny told her all about our "necking" in the woods, and that it was all my idea, and that I was too old for her son, and her son was too innocent for some "wild girl" (that's what she called me, Mom said), and she didn't ever want her son at our house again, and I wasn't ever to go near him, and if Dennis wanted to play with Johnny he would just have to go to their house, but he wasn't ever to bring me!

Then Mom asked me to tell her what happened, and I did. She said that someday I would understand why

Mrs. White got so upset and that I should wait a few years before I practiced kissing any boys again, because kissing is something you have to be careful about. I asked her why, but she just said she would have to think of a good explanation and I should ask her again in a few years. In a few years!

Well, I think that now I know what she meant, but it's sad really, because Johnny and I didn't mean anything by it, and I never got to play with him again. The next time I saw him was about a week later at the drugstore, but he didn't even look at me. He doesn't live on our street anymore and I'll probably never see him again. I haven't kissed (or been kissed by) a boy since, and I do wonder if all lips have no taste, like Johnny's.

Once, when Beth Ann was telling me about Jerry Manelli kissing her at a school dance, I asked her what it tasted like.

"What it *tasted* like?" She looked at me like I was some kind of weirdo.

"Yes, what did it taste like?"

"The kiss?"

"Yes, of course the kiss!"

"Well, nothing."

"You mean it tasted like nothing at all? It must have tasted like *something*." She didn't know about Johnny White and I didn't want to tell her. For some reason, I made it sound like I knew kisses had to taste like a specific thing.

She started fidgeting around. "Well, now that you mention it . . ."

"So it *did* taste like something?"

"Well, yes, it did. . . ."

"Like what? What did it taste like?"

She had her eyes closed as if she was trying to remember, and she was moving her lip around. "Well, I guess it tasted like . . . chicken."

Now that surprised me. "Chicken? Are you sure?"

"Well, gosh, Mary Lou, I wasn't paying that much attention. I think it was like chicken, yes."

It's not the sort of taste you would expect, is it?

Monday, June 18

Maggie spent the entire day gabbing away on the phone. She called Kenny, and then Kenny called her back, and she called her friend Angie and then Angie called her. Back and forth all day. She is cooking up a plan to get Dad to let her go to that party on Saturday. If anyone can do it, Maggie can. It's disgusting. About all she has to do is roll her eyes and talk real sweet and she gets anything she wants.

Ole Carl Ray finally decided he'd get out of his bed around noon. You know, I've never once seen Carl Ray go into the bathroom. Now, I'm sure he must have been in there (well, *really*), but I know for sure he has not taken a shower yet. You can just tell when he walks by. Lord.

He appeared in the kitchen while I was making lunch and stood there watching me. Finally I said, "Are you going to want lunch?" He makes me so mad, the way he stands around waiting for people to feed him and stuff, and lying around not doing a darn thing.

He said, "Okay."

Brother.

While we were eating lunch, I said, "Aren't you going to go out and look for a job?"

He put his sandwich down on his plate and said, to his sandwich it seemed, "Sure."

Well, that was a good sign. "So where are you going?"

Long pause by Carl Ray. Finally he told his sandwich, "Don't rightly know."

"Well," I said to Carl Ray, "didn't you ask Dad for some suggestions?"

"Nope."

"Why not?"

"Don't rightly know."

Tommy started banging on the table with his cup and going, "Ha! Ha!" and then he would look at us and say, “Ha! Ha!” as if he was practicing how to laugh.

In the middle of this, Carl Ray sat there, eating his sandwich in slow motion, chewing and chewing and staring down at his plate as if we weren’t even there.

I said, “You could look in the newspaper.”

“Where’s that at?” he said.

“The newspaper?”

“Yeah.”

I went and got it and showed him where the help wanted section was. “What sort of thing are you looking for?”

“Don’t rightly know.”

“It’s kind of hard to look for a job when you don’t know what you’re looking for, Carl Ray. Maybe you should go downtown and walk along the street and look for signs that say ‘Help Wanted.’ ” He looked up at me and nodded. “You should probably go now, or you won’t have time to see many places.” He nodded. “Do you know how to get downtown?” He didn’t.

So I showed him how to go and told him what he should probably say, and then I told him he should probably change his clothes since he was still wearing the same clothes he had arrived in, and then I told him what sort of clothes to wear, but he said he didn’t have a tie, so I asked him to show me exactly what he did have and it was pitiful: two T-shirts and two pairs of jeans and the shoes he had on.

After he left, I went up and made his stupid bed.

Then I took Tommy and Dougie to the pool, even though it was really Maggie's day to watch Tommy. I could tell she was going to be useless all day, as long as the phone was working. But swimming wasn't bad because Dougie and I were teaching Tommy how to swim and he's so funny. All he really wants to do is jump off the edge and have us catch him. We finally got him to put his head under by missing him a few times.

Beth Ann met us up there. She has a new bathing suit. It's all white and you can tell she thinks she is really something in it. I didn't want to tell her, but you can practically see through it when it's wet. I'll tell her some other time.

While we were sitting on our towels during break time, I looked up and saw, of all people, Alex Cheevey on the outside, leaning against the fence. He was looking at us, so I got up and went over to him.

"You looking for somebody?" I said.

"Oh. Not really."

"Visiting the Murphys again?"

"Huh?"

"Your friends the Murphys—on Winston Road?"

"Oh. Them. Yuh."

"Are they here at the pool?"

Alex looked around. "Don't think so."

"Oh." When I talk with Alex, I always feel like I'm missing something, like I don't hear all the words. "How was the party?"

"Party?"

"Christy's party. Didn't you go?"

"Oh. Yeah. It was okay. Sort of boring."

Alex was wearing these cute blue shorts and a T-shirt with "Ohio State University" printed on it. He asked me who I was with.

"You mean here, at the pool?"

"Yeah."

"Dougie and Tommy, my brothers, well two of them. And Beth Ann. She's over there, see?" Beth Ann was stretched out on her back, with one knee bent and her hand behind her head. She can really overdo it sometimes.

"Do you come here every day?" he asked.

"Well, nearly. Don't they have a pool over where you live?" All of these towns have a community pool, and since we live in Easton, we go to the Easton pool. Alex lives in Norton.

"Oh. Yeah."

"I think you can use a Norton pass here, if you pay twenty-five cents extra. If you wanted to come here, I mean."

"Yeah. Well, I might someday."

And then the whistle blew, meaning break was over, and I had to go watch Tommy or he would drown.

Carl Ray magically appeared at dinnertime again. Just as we were putting the food on the table, in he comes and sits right down in the "special" seat. I suppose he thinks that's his seat now. As usual, he didn't volunteer any information. In fact, he didn't say one word until finally, after Carl Ray had had three helpings of meat loaf, three helpings of corn, and two helpings of potatoes (he would have had more, I bet, but they were all gone), Dad said, "So tell us, Carl Ray, how did the job hunting go?"

Every single one of us looked at Carl Ray, who shrugged his shoulders. We all looked back at Dad, who looked at my mom like it was her turn. She said, "Does that mean you didn't find anything?" We all looked at Carl Ray.

He nodded. He was pretty busy stuffing food into his mouth.

Dad said, "Does that mean yes, you did not find anything?"

Carl Ray nodded again.

It was getting to be like a tennis match, with us all looking down at Carl Ray's end of the table and then back up at Mom and Dad and then back to Carl Ray.

About this time, Maggie makes her move. "Dad, would you like me to get you another glass of water?"

Dad says, "Sure."

Maggie says, "Anything else I can get you while I'm up?"

Dougie says, "Well, I'd like another glass . . ."

But Maggie just glared at him and went in the kitchen. While she was gone, Dennis starts mimicking her, saying, in this real sweet voice, "Mary Louuuuu, is there anything I can get for youuuu?" and then, of course, he starts laughing and I start laughing and my dad tells us to be quiet and watch our manners.

After dinner, I heard Dad talking to Carl Ray about where to look for a job and what to say and how to act when he went in. Carl Ray just listened. Then Dad came into the kitchen and said to Mom, "Doesn't that boy know how to talk?"

Mom said, "Doesn't seem so."

"It could drive a person crazy."

"He's *your* relative."

Dennis and I went out to play spud with Cathy and Barry Furtz. Cathy and Barry are twins and they're Dennis's age. They're pretty nice, but I don't think Mr. Furtz likes it when we play spud in the street. I bet the Furtzes are sorry they moved here. Cathy and Barry had to go in at eight o'clock to take a bath! So Dennis and I just sat on the curb awhile, throwing stones across to the other curb. Carl Ray snuck up on us the way he does. I swear, he's a real spook sometimes. One minute it was just me and Dennis sitting on the curb, and then all of a sudden there was Carl Ray sitting next to Dennis.

Then Mr. Furtz came out with his hose to water the lawn. Last week he offered me fifty cents to do it for him, though I sure don't know why he doesn't pay his own kids to do it. I don't mind, though. Anyway, sure enough, he sees us sitting there and he strolls over and says, "Feel like earning some gold?" That's what he calls fifty cents: gold.

I said, "Sure, Mr. Furtz."

Mr. Furtz is an okay guy. He's sort of funny-looking, all freckly and nearly bald, but he's not that old, I mean he's not an old man, maybe a little younger than my dad. Mr. Furtz bought the hardware store downtown, and when Dennis and I went in there the other day, he let us poke around behind the counter because there weren't many customers in the store.

Carl Ray is intrigued by the strangest things. While I was watering the Furtzes' lawn, Carl Ray snuck up on me and said, "What'd you call him?"

"Who?"

"That man."

"Mr. Furtz?"

Carl Ray said, "Furtz? How do you spell Furtz?" So I told him. "Furtz," he said again. "Furtz."

Weird guy, this Carl Ray.

When we all finally went inside, Maggie was getting Dad a dish of ice cream. She's so obvious. Then she sat on the couch and watched TV with everybody. Usually she doesn't like to do that; she's usually off with her friends or up washing her hair or painting her fingernails or something.

Tuesday, June 19

Not much happened today. About the biggest news is that I took Tommy over to Beth Ann's, and she was strutting all over because her sister Judy is going to introduce her to her boyfriend's brother and the four of them are going to the drive-in on Friday night. Beth Ann is thirteen (well, okay, so she's almost fourteen) years old, not much older than me. Don't you think that's a little *young* to be going to a drive-in with a boy?

Beth Ann is going to be hard to live with after this.

And Carl Ray, by the way, still did not find a job.

Wednesday, June 20

It rained all day.

Beth Ann called to tell me some more about Derek (that's Judy's boyfriend's brother's name). He is five feet seven inches tall, brown hair, and "gorgeous." Beth Ann hasn't seen him yet. That's just what Judy says. Beth Ann must have described every single outfit in her closet, trying to decide what she should wear on Friday night.

Carl Ray, surprise, surprise, did not find a job today.

Thursday, June 21

It is going to be difficult to decide who I should kill first: Maggie, Beth Ann, Dennis, or Carl Ray. To show you what I mean, pretend this is a play.

> *(The scene: The kitchen of a normal house. A thirteen-year-old girl [Mary Lou] is washing the lunch dishes. Her seventeen-year-old sister [Maggie] is on the telephone, which hangs on the wall in the kitchen. A four-year-old boy sits at the kitchen table, splatting his hand in some spilled milk.)*

MAGGIE: *(Pause.)* Oh, Kenny, I'm just so happeeeeee. *(Pause.)* Yes, he did! I thought he might. *(Pause.)* We are still going, aren't we? *(Pause.)* Kenny? *(Pause.)* What do you mean, you're "not sure"? *(Pause. Pause.)*

MARY LOU: Tommy, stop that!

TOMMY: No!

MAGGIE: And what is that supposed to mean? *(Pause.)* You invited Ellen *in case*? *In case?* In case of *what*?

MARY LOU: Tommy, stop that!

TOMMY: Noooo!

MAGGIE: Well, just *un*invite her then. *(Pause.)* Kenny? *(Pause.)* You'll see what you can *do*? *(Pause. Pause. Pause.)*

MARY LOU: Tommy . . .

MAGGIE: Mary Lou, will you be quiet? I'm on the *phone.*

MARY LOU: Surprise, surprise.

MAGGIE: Yes Kenny, I'm still here. *(Pause.)* Fine. *(Sarcastically:)* I'll just sit here and wait for you to let me know! *(She hangs up the phone. To Mary Lou:)* Couldn't you keep quiet for five lousy minutes?

MARY LOU: What's your problem?

MAGGIE: Oh, nothing. My life is just ruined, that's all. *(She runs out of the room, crying.)*

(Tommy continues to splat the milk. The phone rings. Mary Lou answers it.)

MARY LOU: Finney residence, Mary Lou speaking. *(Pause.)* Oh, hi, Beth Ann. *(Pause.)* Oh. *(Pause.)* Really? *(Pause.)* Ah. *(Pause.)* Well . . . *(Pause.)* Maybe . . . *(Long pause.)* The blue blouse and the white skirt. *(Pause.)* Oh. *(Pause.)* Ah. *(Pause.)* The red blouse. . . . *(Pause.)* Oh. *(Long pause.)* Uh-huh. *(Pause.)* Yup. *(Pause.)* Glad I could be of some help. *(She hangs up the phone.)*

(Tommy continues to splat the milk. The phone rings. Mary Lou answers it.)

MARY LOU: Finney residence, Mary Lou speak— *(Pause.)* Oh, hello, Beth Ann.

(Mary Lou's brother Dennis, age twelve, enters, running, and stops behind Mary Lou, where he proceeds to pull on the phone cord and make faces.)

MARY LOU: Stop it! *(Pause.)* No, I meant Dennis. Stop it! *(Dennis doesn't stop it.)* He's pulling on the stupid cord. *(Pause.)* Oh. The green blouse. . . . *(Pause.)* Ah. Stop it! *(Pause.)* No, I meant Dennis. He's still pull— *(Pause.)* Oh, God. *(Pause.)* No, I'm not mad.

DENNIS: *(putting his mouth by the phone)* You're just jeallllll-ous, Mar-eee Louuuuu.

MARY LOU: *(pushes Dennis away)* Will you just STOP it? *(Pause.)* No, I meant . . . *(Pause.)* No, I am NOT jealous. . . .

(Scene fades out. Next scene opens as family is finishing dinner. Mary Lou, Maggie, Tommy, Dennis, their mother, their father, another brother—Dougie, age eight—and a cousin named Carl Ray, age seventeen, are at the table.)

DENNIS: *(to no one in particular)* Mary Lou is jealous 'cause Beth Ann has a DATE.

MARY LOU: Be quiet.

MOTHER: Is that true, Mary Lou?

MARY LOU: NO! God.

MOTHER: Don't say "God." Beth Ann doesn't have a date?

DENNIS: She does too.

MOTHER: Well, does she or doesn't she, Mary Lou? Dennis, stop poking Dougie.

FATHER: Carl Ray, did you get a job today?

CARL RAY: Un-uh.

FATHER: Does that mean no, you didn't?

CARL RAY: Uh-huh.

FATHER: Does that mean yes it's right that no . . . *(He stops, looks at mother. He seems to be in pain.)*

(Scene fades to kitchen, where Mary Lou and Maggie are washing dishes while mother puts things in refrigerator.)

MOTHER: Mary Lou, I want to talk to you about Carl Ray's room.

(Mary Lou keeps washing the dishes.)

MOTHER: His bed looks like Tommy made it up.
MARY LOU: He did.
MOTHER: *Tommy* made it up?
MARY LOU: Yup.
MOTHER: And why was that?
MARY LOU: What?
MOTHER: Why did Tommy make up Carl Ray's bed?
MARY LOU: Don't rightly know.
MOTHER: Mary Lou Finney . . .
MARY LOU: Okay, okay. Tommy made it up because I asked him to because I am sick and tired of cleaning up after that . . .

MOTHER: Mary Lou Finney, *you* will make up our guest's bed and *you* will clean his room. For the first two weeks he's a guest. Remember?

(Mother leaves room.)

MARY LOU: Brother.

(The phone rings. Maggie practically breaks her neck running to answer it.)

MAGGIE: Finney residence, Maggie speaking. *(Pause.)* Oh, Angie . . . *(Pause.)* You talked to Ellen? Oh, good. What did she— *(Pause.)* And you told her about me and Kenny. . . . *(Pause.)* Oh, good. She is? He did? Oh, good. *(Pause.)* Okay, 'bye. *(She hangs up, smiles. The phone rings and Maggie grabs it.)*

MAGGIE: Finney residence, Mag— *(Pause. Sweetly.)* Oh, hello Kenny. *(Pause.)* You did? *(Pause.)* You do? *(Pause.)* Well . . . *(Pause.)* I guess so.

(Scene fades out.)

And that's just the way the day went.

Friday, June 22

Right now Beth Ann is probably still out on her big date. I'm going to have to hear every little detail tomorrow. Today I stopped over at her house and she modeled about fifteen outfits, still trying to decide what she was going to wear. Honestly, I don't see what all the fuss is about. Guys never notice anyway. She finally decided on a red blouse and white slacks. I thought she looked a little fat in that outfit, but she was such a wreck that I didn't dare say so.

Then she messed around with her hair for about three hours, trying to decide whether it looked better up or down. At about four o'clock she said she had to take a bath and start getting ready. Derek and his brother were arriving at seven! I sure hope she had enough time.

Maybe I *am* a little jealous, but also I am sort of happy for her, because she thinks this is such a big deal. I don't think *I* would want to go out with someone I had never met before, though. I mean, what if you didn't like the guy?

I guess you could probably tell from the play I wrote yesterday that dear ole Maggie got permission from Dad to go to the big party on Saturday with Kenny. Cinderella Maggie has to be home at midnight, though.

Today was Maggie's day to watch Tommy, but she traded with me because she had to go out and buy a dress. Brother. She came home with this skin-eeee black dress that has almost no back.

I think Carl Ray is putting on a few pounds (no wonder). Maybe he didn't get fed at Aunt Radene's. The biggest news of the day came at dinner, when Dad said, for about the millionth time, "So, Carl Ray, find a job today?"

Carl Ray *nodded*. We almost missed it, because we are so used to him saying "Un-uh" or "Nope."

Dad said, "Does that mean . . ."

Mom said, "You got a . . ."

And for the first time since Carl Ray arrived, he actually grinned. "Yup," he said.

Boy, did Dad look happy. "Well, now, that's great news!"

"Sure is, Carl Ray," I said, and all around the table everyone was saying "Wow" and "Good" and "My, my."

Carl Ray kept grinning. He actually had to stop shoveling food into his mouth because he was grinning so much. This is how it went after that:

DAD: So where is this new job?

CARL RAY: Hardware store.

MOM: Furtz's Hardware?

CARL RAY: Yup.

DAD: Well!

MOM: And what will you do there?

CARL RAY: *(after a pause)* Don't rightly know.

DAD: You don't know what your job entails?

CARL RAY: *(after a pause)* Un-uh.

MAGGIE: When do you start work, Carl Ray?

CARL RAY: Monday.

Do we sound like a boring family or what?

Well, anyway, at least Carl Ray found a job and at least he knows when he *starts.*

Saturday, June 23

I can hardly believe it, but I've almost filled up this whole journal and I've only been writing two weeks! I went out and bought another one today because I like doing this. It makes it easier to go to bed at night, for some reason.

Today was your regular Saturday: Got up late, good ole Alesci's ham and hot bread for lunch (this time Mom didn't make us wait for Carl Ray to hog it all first), waited around for Master Carl Ray to get up so I could make up his stupid bed (seven more days of this slavery), watched

Carl Ray sit in front of the TV, went over to Beth Ann's.

Beth Ann was acting as if she'd just been crowned the Queen of Easton or something. I'd never seen her like that. When I went over there, she was lying on her bed dressed in one of her sister Judy's flimsy nightgowns (pink nylon! aaargh), flipping through *Seventeen*. She didn't even seem happy to see me.

"Oh, hi there," she said. She kept flipping through the magazine.

"Welllll?"

She turned a page. "Do you like this outfit?" She held it up for me to see.

"Not really."

"Hmm." She flipped to the next page.

"Welllll?" I was beginning to feel a little invisible.

"Hmm?" She was studying an underwear ad.

"Aren't you going to tell me about last night?" Normally she would have been pouring out every single detail even if she and her parents had gone to the Tast-ee Freeze.

"Oh." She put the magazine down and stretched out on the bed, fixing the nightgown as if someone was going to take her picture. Then she got this dreamy look on her face and said, "It was di-viiiiine."

Di-viiiiine? Did she say *di-viiiiine*?

"Derek is truly wonderful."

Truly? Where did she get these words like divine and truly?

"He's truly precious."

Truly precious. I thought I was going to gag. She sounded just like Christy and Megan at school. "Beth Ann, just tell me what you did, huh? Did you go to the drive-in?"

She nodded and got this big smile on her face.

"With Judy and what's-his-name?"

"Gregory. Derek's brother's name is Gregory."

"Okay, with Judy and Gregory?"

"Yes."

This was driving me crazy. Beth Ann (normally) would tell you what everyone wore and what color the car was and what color the interior of the car was and if it was clean or dirty, and then she would get on to what time he picked her up and what her mother said and what her father said and on and on and on.

Then she sat up and said, "So what are you doing tonight?"

"Nothing. Want to go to the movies or something?"

She started winding a piece of her hair around her finger. "Oh, I'd love to, Mary Lou, but I can't. Derek and I are going to some party with Judy and Gregory."

I went home. It really bothered me all day that she didn't tell me anything about her date and that she dropped that bit about her and Derek going out again, dropped it like some big bomb right on my head. I didn't think best friends did that sort of thing.

Even though our house was full of people all day, I kept having this lonely feeling. It was really strange. Am I jealous?

I'll probably never have a date. I'll probably go on and on watching Maggie and Beth Ann be all soppy over boys and I'll probably wake up one day and be seventy-five years old in my wheelchair, with drool running down my chin, and I will still not ever have been on a date.

It didn't help matters that Maggie spent the entire day soaking in the tub and doing her nails and fixing her hair. I have to admit, though, that she looked terrific when she got ready to go.

When Kenny came to pick her up, he came into the house and sat down (he never sits down) and pretended to talk like an adult to my father.

He said, "Hello, Mr. Finney, sir."

My dad just sort of smiled. "Hello, Kenny."

"Have you had a nice day, Mr. Finney, uh, sir?"

"Yes."

Kenny kept turning his head. I think his collar was too small. He was all dressed up in a gray suit and a white shirt and a blue tie.

"So where exactly is this party?" my dad asked.

"Oh, yes, sir, it's at the Fergusons'. Do you know Bill Ferguson?"

"No, I don't think I do."

"Well, he's a very nice guy. You'd like him, Mr. Finney. Well, I think you might."

"And where exactly does this Bill Ferguson live?"

"Oh, he lives in this big house over in Norton. Seven-three-three Lindale Street. Here's the phone number. I wrote it down for you."

My dad looked at the piece of paper Kenny gave him. "Hmmm."

So they went on like that until Maggie came downstairs and everybody fell all over her saying how terrific she looked. Carl Ray kept staring at her as if she was some sort of goddess or something. And, of course, Dad reminded her to be home by midnight and Kenny right away said, "Oh, of course, sir. Midnight it is. Very good."

It's now eleven o'clock. I wonder what time she'll really be home.

Sunday, June 24

Well! Would any-one in this world be surprised to learn that Maggie got home at two o'clock? And that she's not even in trouble? Cinderella called around midnight and asked for an extension.

But I found out a lot of stuff from Maggie today! I asked her about the party and for once she decided to talk to me and she told me all about it. It was *very* fancy, she said, with butlers and maids. They had all kinds of little things to eat like dips and mushrooms and there was a live band that played outside on the patio and everyone danced and the neighbors didn't even complain.

The thing that surprised me the most was when she said that Beth Ann was there! And then, after Maggie made me PROMISE not to tell, she said that Beth Ann was hanging allllllll over Derek-the-Divine, and that Derek was "sort of a jerk." She said, "He's just sort of gawky and his eyes sort of bug out so he always looks surprised and he didn't say two words, just sort of followed Judy and what's-his-name around, and Beth Ann followed *him* around."

Then, out of the blue, Maggie said, "Oh, funny, I just remembered that there was some guy there who asked about you."

"Meeee? Somebody asked about *me*?"

"Now what was his name? He lives next door to Bill Ferguson—the guy who had the party. That's probably why he was there. I don't think he had a date, and I only saw him there at the beginning."

"You don't remember his *name*?" Maggie never

remembers names. It's exasperating. "Describe him, then," I said.

"Well. He's pretty cute, sort of tallish and thinnish, blondish hair, with pinkish skin . . ."

"Alex? Was it Alex Cheevey? He lives in Norton and he has this sort of pinkish . . ."

"Alex! That's it. Yes, Alex."

Alex Cheevey was at the party. And he asked about me. Well, sort of. And Beth Ann's "truly divine wonderful gorgeous Derek" is sort of a jerk.

I felt a lot better today.

Monday, June 25

This is the first day of the new journal, but I'm not going to write much because I am sooooo sleepy.

I had to watch Tommy all afternoon even though it was supposed to be Maggie's day (she traded Friday with me), but Mr. Furtz is sick. He came home early from the store and Mrs. Furtz had to take him to the doctor, so Maggie had to go over there and stay with Cathy, Barry, and David. Mrs. Furtz didn't get home until eight, and she was all upset because the doctor said Mr. Furtz should go right into the hospital for some tests.

Maggie's going to go over again tomorrow so Mrs.

Furtz can go to the hospital. The surprising thing is that Mr. Furtz looks like one of those real healthy types—he plays lots of golf and tennis and is always running around in his gym shorts and tennis shoes. He's got these really long skinny legs and great big feet. Mom says she bets he's home in a couple days and these doctors are always scaring people with tests for every little thing.

I don't much like doctors, because they never really listen to you, but I guess it must be hard to sit there and listen to people complain all day.

I still haven't heard from Beth Ann, and I decided I wasn't going to call her. I'll wait till *she* wants to talk to *me*.

Oh, I guess I better tell about Carl Ray. Dad had to call him about a thousand times this morning to get him out of bed for his first day of work, but he finally did get up. Then at dinner, when Dad asked how his job was, Carl Ray said, "Enhh."

And surprisingly, Dad didn't say, "Does that mean . . . ?" Instead he said, "Well, good. I'm glad to hear it." I think he's getting sort of fed up with Carl Ray. Mom asked Carl Ray if someone took over for Mr. Furtz at the store while he was at the doctor's, and Carl Ray said, "Yup," but he never said who it was.

When I was cleaning Carl Ray's room today, I put a can of deodorant on his dresser. Har har har. Is that mean? Well, it was just supposed to be a hint.

Good night, whoever you are out there.

Tuesday, June 26

Mr. Furtz is still in the hospital. He had a bunch of tests, but no results yet, and he has to have some more tests tomorrow. Maggie said that Mrs. Furtz is a wreck. I'm sure Mr. Furtz will be home soon.

No word from my best friend, Beth Ann.

Do you want to know how Carl Ray's job went today? Well, at dinner, when Mom asked him, he said, "Ehhh."

I examined the can of deodorant today, but I couldn't tell if it had been used. So I added a new bar of soap to his dresser top. Har har har.

Today, in the mail, we all got our summer reading lists for school. On it are about a million books for each grade and you're supposed to read "as many as possible," and then take notes.

Tommy and I went to the library today. He picked out a bunch of easy-reader books (he can't read yet, but he pretends) and a book on Eskimos (Eskimos???). I checked out two on the list: the *Odyssey* and *Poems of Robert Frost*.

I skimmed through the *Odyssey* and think perhaps I

made a mistake getting this one. The print is so small (I hate that) and there's all these weird names in it. Maybe I'll try reading it tomorrow.

I read a couple poems in the Robert Frost book. Some are okay, but some are very strange, like the one in the front about a pasture. Someone is going out to the pasture and tells someone else to come along too. That's about it, really. I wrote a poem once about a lunch box and a bologna (why is that word spelled like that?) sandwich, and I think even *that* was better than the one about the pasture.

Wednesday, June 27

The worst thing happened today.

After dinner, Mom and I were in the kitchen (Maggie was still over at the Furtzes') and the phone rang. Mom answered it and I heard her suck in her breath and then say, "Oh, no," and "How?" and "When?" I just knew it was some kind of bad news.

When she hung up, she ran right upstairs calling, "Sam, Sam, Sam." My dad met her at the top of the stairs, and she said, "Oh, Sam. That new neighbor—Mr. Furtz—he's *dead*."

She told my dad that she had just talked to Maggie,

who had just talked to Mrs. Furtz, who was still at the hospital and practically hysterical, so Maggie didn't find out too much except that Mr. Furtz had been resting after some tests and he was supposed to come home tomorrow. Mrs. Furtz was waiting out in the hall while a nurse was doing something in there, and all of a sudden this light started flashing over his door and all these people started running in and out and Mrs. Furtz thought it was his roommate who was in trouble because she had just seen her husband and he was fine.

Then a nurse asked Mrs. Furtz to come down the hall with her, and they took her into a room and fifteen minutes later they told her that Mr. Furtz was dead.

He had a gigantic heart attack or something.

I just can't believe it.

My mom and dad had only met Mr. Furtz once, but they went right over to the Furtzes' to wait for Mrs. Furtz to come home.

I keep wondering about Cathy and Barry and little David (who is Tommy's age). What is their mother going to tell them?

I don't feel like writing about other stuff just now, because it doesn't seem right. It's scary that a person can be as healthy-looking as Mr. Furtz and then, boom, all of a sudden he isn't here anymore. I'm glad Mrs. Furtz was visiting Mr. Furtz just before it happened. Maybe she was holding his hand or something. I don't much like it, though, that Mrs. Furtz wasn't in the room when all the lights started flashing. That's probably when Mr. Furtz needed his wife the most. Maybe he wanted to tell her one last thing.

And what about Mrs. Furtz standing out there in the hallway, not expecting this to happen? And what about his children and his friends and neighbors who are just going along, doing the dishes and stuff and then all of a sudden the telephone rings and you think it's going to be some regular person calling with some regular ole chatter, and wham, it's the most awful news.

And I also keep wondering about my mom and dad. They seem so healthy too. Please, please, please don't let anything happen to them.

Thursday, June 28

Oh Lord, I don't like this dead Mr. Furtz business *at all.*

Maggie and I went over to the Furtzes' today to see if we could take Cathy, Barry, and David out somewhere, just to get them out of the house. About a hundred (well, maybe twenty) relatives were swarming all over. They said Mrs. Furtz had to go pick out a coffin. Can you *imagine* that? With your husband dead and all, they make you go pick out a coffin. How do you do that? Is there a room with a bunch of coffins and you just choose one? Do you choose one because it is pretty or because it is sturdy and won't, sort of, *leak*? What if you don't have enough money for a good, leakproof coffin?

Cathy and Barry were up in their rooms playing Monopoly with their cousins. At first I thought it was strange that they were sitting there buying hotels and trading property when their father was dead and their mother was out shopping around for a coffin, but then I couldn't imagine what they *should* be doing. Maybe crying and looking at some pictures of him or something. Cathy and Barry didn't want to go anywhere because they wanted to finish Monopoly.

Little David Furtz was sitting at the kitchen table playing with some Play-Doh. When I asked him what he was making, he said, "Sort of a squirrel."

I peered at it and it even looked like a squirrel, so I said, "That's a great squirrel."

And do you know what he said? He said, "It's for Daddy."

His uncle, who was sitting at the table watching David, whispered, "He doesn't understand."

Then David shouted, "I do *too*!" and he punched the

little squirrel flat and ran out of the room.

Tonight, Mom said that there would be a "viewing" (of the *body*!) tomorrow night at DiMaggio's Funeral Home, which is about two blocks from our house.

"Can we go?" I asked. I've never seen a body before. Except on TV.

Mom looked at Dad. He said, "Hmm."

"Maybe they should, Sam," my mom said.

"Hmm."

"Oh, pleeeease," said Dennis.

"Well, I'm not going!" said Maggie.

"I wanna go!" said Tommy. He didn't even know where we were going.

Carl Ray, of course, didn't say anything. He must have been wondering if he was still going to have a job now, with Mr. Furtz dead and all.

"Well, fine then. You can come, but behave yourselves."

So we're all going tomorrow. Except for Maggie and Carl Ray, I guess.

Beth Ann finally called. Surprise, surprise. She said she was sorry she hadn't called sooner, but she's been so *busy*. I didn't ask her what she was busy doing.

She asked me what I was doing tomorrow night. Well, I've fallen for that one before, so I was happy that I had something to say. "Going to the funeral home,"

I said. I knew she'd be surprised. She wanted to know who was there, and I told her it was Mr. Furtz, our new neighbor. She asked if he was dead. Of course he was dead, I told her.

I feel terrible about Mr. Furtz. I keep expecting to see him outside, puttering around his yard. I told my parents they ought to take some vitamins.

Here's some *Odyssey* notes to take my mind off Mr. Furtz. I'll write them in red ink.

Sacking Cities

I tried to read the Odyssey *today, but I couldn't get past the first couple of pages. Homer writes so strangely. He begins, "Tell me, O Muse, of that ingenious hero who traveled far and wide after he had sacked the famous town of Troy." Doesn't that sound a little much?*

Fortunately, I knew what a Muse was from English last year. A Muse is a goddess who sits around inspiring people whenever she feels like it. If you're telling a story and don't feel too inspired, you're supposed to call on the Muse for help. It looks like Homer needed some help right from the start. If I were Homer, I don't think I'd admit that right at the beginning of the story.

And then I just can't warm right up to a character who is a hero (an ingenious *hero) because he "sacked" a town! Lord.*

Homer also has a strange way of putting things. For example, instead of saying, "He visited many cities," Homer will say, "Many cities did he visit." It reminds me of the preacher at Aunt Radene's church in West Virginia. He would make his voice really soft and then, boom, he would be shouting and then soft again. And he would say things like "Many people did our Jesus cure," and "Little did He know." You could tell that this preacher really liked to talk and that he was really proud of what he said and the way he said it.

Anyway, about all I can make out from the first part of the Odyssey *is that it's going to be about this man Odysseus who "sacked" Troy and then started on his way home but all these gods are trying to decide if they should let Odysseus get started on his journey home to his wife. Then you find out that back at his wife's house a bunch of men are falling all over her, waiting for the opportunity to marry her. It's like a soap opera!*

It just kills me the way these gods decide everything. Here's this big hero Odysseus and everything he does is because the gods decide he should do it.

I keep wondering if there are still all these gods like Zeus and Athene and Poseidon sitting around up there on Mount Olympus deciding if I should go to Mr. Furtz's funeral or, even worse, deciding when it was time for Mr. Furtz to die. Are they saying, "Should Mary Lou Finney die today?"

"Well, yes, I think she should, because many people has she slighted of late."

"Well, I don't agree," says another one. "She's a good kid. Let us halt awhile." Etc.

Also, I have trouble keeping track of all the names. In the first three pages, just to give you an idea of why I have trouble, here are the names mentioned: Hyperion, Zeus, Odysseus, Calypso, Poseidon, Ethiopians, Aegisthus, Agamemnon, Orestes, Hermes, Athene, Cronus, Atlas, Polyphemus, Cyclopes, Thoosa, Phorcys, Telemachus, Penelope, Mentes, Taphians.

I was reading this in the living room after dinner while Carl Ray was watching TV, and I got so frustrated, I just threw the book down and said, "Telemachus! Who the heck is Telemachus?"

And do you know what Carl Ray did? He said, without even looking away from the TV, "The son of Odysseus."

You could have knocked me over with a feather. "And

how do *you* know *that*?" I asked.

"Simple," he said, and he kept right on watching *The Dating Game.*

I didn't even think Carl Ray knew how to *read*.

Friday, June 29

I will never forget tonight as long as I live (and hey, Zeus, I would like that to be quite a bit longer, please).

We viewed Mr. Furtz tonight.

I don't know where to start. I never expected anything like this. First of all, DiMaggio's Funeral Home is really like a *home* inside. I guess I thought it would be like a hospital with green walls and tile floors and people in white coats. But it was like a house, with a living room where people were standing around talking. There were lamps and tables and couches and all that. When I saw the living room, I thought for a minute that they were going to have Mr. Furtz propped up in a chair with a newspaper in his lap. Dentist-office music was playing in the background.

Oh, I forgot to mention that, surprise, surprise, guess who came along with us. Carl Ray! None of us could believe it when we were walking down the street (like I said, the funeral home is only two blocks away) and all of a sudden Dougie said, "Hey, there's Carl Ray!" We all turned around, and sure enough, Carl Ray was following right behind us.

"Now that's one strange boy," my father whispered to my mother.

Anyway, Dennis started pulling on my arm at the funeral home, and Carl Ray said, "Come on." I don't know why I was so surprised to see Carl Ray lead the way, but we followed him. We went through some curtains and there it was.

The coffin. It was sitting up on a table and it was *open*! Dennis said, "Whooaa." Carl Ray stepped right up and pulled Dennis beside him. Dennis dragged me.

I couldn't breathe. There was Mr. Furtz, lying on this white silky pillow with his hands folded over his chest. He was wearing a brown suit and a white dress shirt and tie. And he had this fancy quilt over him, covering his legs. It seemed strange to see a man in a suit lying in this box that was trying to look like a bed.

He really did look like he was sleeping, and he looked pretty much like Mr. Furtz except he wasn't smiling as he usually did, and his face looked like it had powder on it. I kept thinking he was going to open his eyes and be real mad that we were all staring at him.

I never saw so many flowers all in one room before. There were flowers in the coffin ("To Charles Randolph

Furtz, With love from your children"), baskets of gladiolas all along a shelf behind the coffin, and then about a hundred other baskets of flowers around the room.

I started looking at these baskets, because each one had a card on it telling who it was from. The cards said things like "In loving memory" and "Rest in peace" and "To our Beloved." They were all pretty depressing. It was as if people were cramming in all these last-minute messages in case Mr. Furtz could still hear. The funny thing was he looked as if he *could* hear. I kept looking at the cards, wishing at least one of them would say the truth: "Oh how awful!" or "I wish you weren't dead" or "This is the absolute worst thing in the world." But none of them did.

When I turned around to show Dennis, Carl Ray was staring down into the coffin and rubbing his finger over this brass marker on the side of the coffin. The marker had Mr. Furtz's initials on it: CRF. But then I saw Carl Ray reach out with one hand and touch Mr. Furtz on the arm! "Carl Ray!" I said.

He jumped back. And then you know what? Carl Ray was *crying*! I have to admit that I felt like crying as soon as I saw Mr. Furtz, but Carl Ray hardly knows him. For a minute there, I actually *liked* Carl Ray because he could cry over Mr. Furtz like that.

I saw my mom standing by Dad, and they were both

crying. I don't think I've ever seen my dad cry, and that made me so sad.

They told us kids to go on home, because they were going to stay awhile, so we started back up the street. I was surprised to see that Carl Ray was holding Tommy's hand.

"Did you see the body?" Dougie asked Tommy.

Tommy nodded. His eyes were wide open—you could tell he didn't like what he saw. Then Tommy turned to Carl Ray and said, "So where's he going now?"

"They'll bury him," Carl Ray said.

"Where?"

"In the cemetery, in the ground."

"Does he stay in the box?"

"Yup."

"What about heaven?"

Carl Ray looked up at the sky and back at Tommy. "What about it?"

"When does he go there?"

"Well," Carl Ray said, "soon, I guess."

Tommy was staring at Carl Ray's face real hard. "So how is he gonna get out of the ground?"

Carl Ray didn't even bat an eye. "God will come and get his soul."

Tommy nodded.

All of a sudden, I saw this image of Zeus swooping

down with this shovel and digging down into the earth and pulling open the coffin and taking Mr. Furtz by the hand and flying off with him up into the clouds, sort of like Superman. Imagine.

But now that I am home and it's dark outside and time to go to bed, I just don't like the idea of Mr. Furtz being in that box when they close the lid, and of him being down there in the ground while Mrs. Furtz and Cathy and Barry and David go on living in that house.

And I keep wondering what Mr. Furtz *feels* like. I know, I know, he can't feel anything if he's dead, but he must know it's dark or that he can't breathe or that everyone is crying and feeling so miserable that he's gone. Can he dream? Is he just waiting for someone to come and take his soul?

Saturday, June 30

Mr. Furtz was buried today. Only Mom and Dad went. They decided that none of us kids could go because we all had nightmares last night (all except Carl Ray, who if he did have one didn't admit it, and Maggie, who didn't go to the funeral home).

In my dream (or nightmare) I was walking through these woods. It was snowing and very cold and I was lost. I kept looking for my parents, calling, "Mom! Dad!" There were no tracks anywhere and it was pretty dark. I thought I saw Carl Ray behind a tree, and I called his name and ran up to the tree, but when I got there he was gone. I was screaming, "Carl Ray! Save me! Save me!" And then I sat up straight in bed and there was Maggie staring at me, saying, "Hey! Wake up!"

Dennis said he dreamed that someone locked him in the garage and people kept staring in the window but he couldn't hear what they were saying and they wouldn't let him out.

Dougie said he was picking flowers in this huge field of flowers when all of a sudden a big black bird came down out of the sky and started pecking at his head.

And Tommy said the "boogerman" was after him, so he climbed in bed with Mom and Dad, and then he wet the bed, which *really* made Dad mad.

Nobody felt like doing anything today while Mom and Dad were gone. When Tommy said he was hungry for lunch, I realized that Dad wouldn't be going to Alesci's today, so I started rummaging through the cupboards for something to fix. And then, what do you know? In walks Carl Ray (up before noon on Saturday for the first time since he arrived) with a big Alesci's bag. He had walked all the way there (about a mile) and back. He had just what we needed: hot bread and ham. It made me feel a little bad about the deodorant and the soap I left on his dresser.

Oh, I forgot to mention yesterday that Beth Ann didn't come over. She had to go get her hair cut (all day?). But she did come over this afternoon for about an hour. She seemed real curious about Carl Ray. She kept asking what he was like and where he worked and what I thought of him and which room was his and didn't we *mind* him staying there and how long was he staying and on and on. She sure can talk.

It was funny, but even though Carl Ray has not been the most thrilling guest and he has sure driven me crazy, I didn't tell Beth Ann any of that. In fact I made him sound almost *exotic*. Carl Ray! And when she asked if we minded him staying there, I said, "Beth Ann! What a thing to say. Of course we don't *mind*—where else would he stay?" even though we all mind a whole lot, especially me.

Finally, I had to ask Beth Ann about Derek. "So how's Derek?" I asked.

She looked down at her fingernails before answering. "Ohhh, he's just fiiiiine."

"So what does he look like?"

"Oh, he's just gorgeous!"

"I know, but what does he *look* like?"

"Well, he has these cute blue eyes and these longgggg eyelashes and this adorrrrr-able smile."

"Ah. I can just picture him." Actually, I couldn't at all. Her description wasn't exactly precise. "Is he gawky?"

"*Gawky? Gawky!* No!"

"Does he talk?"

"Of course he does, Mary Lou. You make it sound like you think he's some sort of jerk or something." She has a way of pulling down her mouth on the sides like a little kid who's letting you know you've hurt her feelings.

I really wanted to know what they *did* at these movies. I mean, did they just sit there or did they talk or hold hands or what? But I figured that was the kind of thing she would tell me without my having to ask. She didn't, though. She seems like she's bragging more when she *doesn't* tell me what happened than if she *did* tell me all the details.

I'm still plodding along in the *Odyssey*. I'll switch pens.

Magic Sandals

I think I like the goddess Athene (in English class we always said Athena, but it's spelled Athene here) the best so far. She has these flashy magical sandals that enable her to fly, and she also has a spear, and she can disguise herself as a man or woman. At the end of the first "book" (a book is more like a chapter), she just flies away. Now, wouldn't you love to do that?

The second book was all about Odysseus's wife, Penelope, and his son, Telemachus, and all the suitors (the guys after Penelope) hanging around. Some of them talk on and on and on, sort of like Beth Ann.

Anyway, Telemachus decides to go off in search of his father (Odysseus), who everyone thinks is dead (he's been gone ten or twenty years, I think) and Athene swoops down and disguises herself and gives Telemachus lots of help, telling him what to do and putting the suitors into a deep sleep and finding a ship and crew for him and then even giving him a good wind. Geez. Wouldn't you like to have your own personal Athene? Someone to solve all your problems?

Sunday, July 1

How can it be July already???

Tell me, O Muse, of something to write. Inspire me.

I'm waiting, O Muse.

I think my Muse is attending some other people at the moment.

So. Today is Sunday and everyone is still moping around about Mr. Furtz. There's a big wreath hanging on the Furtzes' door, sort of like a Christmas wreath only not so cheery. It sure looks strange to see it hanging there in the middle of summer. The Furtzes' curtains were drawn closed the whole day and cars kept going in and out of the driveway.

All day it rained. Dougie said it was God crying about Mr. Furtz, but I told him that if that was true and if God cried every time someone died, it would rain every single day. But it's a nice thought, about God crying, I mean. I keep thinking about Mr. Furtz lying there in that box and that lid closing on him.

I don't think my parents are taking their vitamins. It scares me half to death.

Snoring Through the **Odyssey**

I read Book Three of the Odyssey *today. Snore, snore, snore. Telemachus is still off trying to find out what happened to his father (he thinks he's dead).*

There were a couple of interesting things in this section, though. First, Athene says something about death. When a man's time comes (to die), she says, no one can help him, not even a god. It made it sound like there's a set time, all prearranged or something.

Spooky. Why was Mr. Furtz's time so early? The other interesting thing was that Athene changes into an eagle and flies away. Imagine everyone's surprise. What an exit!

One other thing I like in this book is the way Homer describes the sun coming up. He doesn't just say, "The sun came up." He says "rosy-fingered Dawn appeared," and he also calls Dawn the "child of morning." It makes you think of this little baby with pink fingers crawling up over the horizon.

I rummaged around in the attic today. Found my father's ice skates, which must be about three thousand years old, and his high-school yearbook (what a scream) and lots of old pictures. There was one of Dad, Uncle Carl Joe, and Aunt Radene. They all looked so young and happy. In this picture, Aunt Radene is standing to one side of Dad and Uncle Carl Joe, leaning against a tree, and it looks as if she is dreaming about something wonderful, because she has this little smile on her face and she isn't looking right at the camera. She is wearing a halter top and very short shorts and high heels. Her hair is long and curly. Carl Ray sure did not get his looks from his mother.

When I made up Carl Ray's stupid bed and cleaned his stupid room today, I left a note that said, "Maid service ends TODAY at 11.00 a.m." The two weeks are up! Carl Ray has to make his own stupid bed from now on.

Called Beth Ann but she was out with Derek-the-Di-viiiiine.

What a day, eh?

Monday, July 2

My Muse has utterly abandoned me.

Tuesday, July 3

Well, Maggie suckered me into watching Tommy today even though I thought it was her turn. But in a way it was a good thing, because I took Tommy to the pool and guess who showed up—Alex Cheevey!

He actually swam around and stuff. Even though I had to stay with Tommy in the shallow end, Alex came and played with Tommy awhile. Alex was in a pretty good mood. He sat with us during break time and let Tommy jump on his stomach. He also talked a little, although it was tough going at times. For instance, it went something like this:

ME: So are you visiting the Murphys again?

ALEX: *(Laughing a little.)* Huh. Huh. Yep.

ME: What, don't they have any kids or anything?

ALEX: Who?

ME: The Murphys.

ALEX: Oh. Nope.

ME: So you got bored and came to the pool?

ALEX: Me? Oh. Yup.

ME: Do you like the Murphys?

ALEX: Me? Oh. Yup.

(A little later.)

ME: Hey, I heard you were at Bill Ferguson's party last week.

ALEX: Yup.

ME: Do you know him? *(Stupid question!)*

ALEX: Yup. Lives next door.

ME: How was it?

ALEX: What?

ME: The party!

ALEX: Oh. Okay. I saw your sister there. *(That's a lot of words for Alex.)*

ME: Yeah, I know. Was it fun?

ALEX: The party?

ME: Yes, the party.

ALEX: Sort of. Why didn't you go? *(He actually asked a question.)*

ME: I wasn't invited.

ALEX: Oh.

(A little later.)

ME: Our neighbor died.

ALEX: Really?

ME: Yeah.

ALEX: Was he sick?

ME: No, not exactly.

ALEX: Well, how did he die?

ME: Well, I guess he was sick only no one knew it. He went in the hospital for some tests and died of some gigantic heart attack or something.

ALEX: Ugh.

ME: Yeah, I know.

ALEX: He didn't think he was sick?

ME: No. I don't think so. At least not until they told him he had to go in for some tests. His time was up. I hate that.

ALEX: Ugh.

ME: Yeah.

ALEX: Yup.

ME: I wonder if he knew he was going to die.

ALEX: Maybe.

ME: Like maybe he had this feeling . . .

ALEX: Maybe.

ME: You ought to at least have a feeling . . .

ALEX: Yup.

ME: Wouldn't you like to have a little advance notice if you were going to kick off?

ALEX: Yup. I would.

ME: Me, too.

And that's all we talked about because he had to leave, but he said he was coming back again on Thursday probably. I might go swimming on Thursday.

Carl Ray still has a job, even though Mr. Furtz is dead. Mr. Furtz's brother (whose name is also Furtz, of course) is going to take over the store at least for a while. I found that out when I went to the hardware store today. I didn't really need to buy something, but I was downtown with Tommy after swimming and I just wanted to see if it was possible that Carl Ray could really do anything useful.

When we went in, there was Carl Ray dusting off some turpentine cans. He looked real embarrassed to see us at first, but Tommy took hold of Carl Ray's hand and was so excited to see him that Carl Ray eventually smiled a little and started acting like he owned the store, showing us all around. I've been to that store a million times, so I'd seen it all before, but I pretended like I hadn't. Then the new Mr. Furtz came up and introduced himself ("Gene Furtz here") and said he was taking over the store at least temporarily, until "things settle down."

Then he said, "Don't you worry, we'll keep young Carl Ray on here." (I wasn't worried.) Carl Ray smiled and looked down at his shoes. What a presence.

Stopped at Beth Ann's on the way home, but she was gone.

Anointing Telemachus

Read Book Four of the Odyssey. *Now Telemachus is at Menelaus's house, where everybody is feasting and "making merry." It really kills me how everyone treats Telemachus wherever he goes. He's a total stranger and yet Menelaus orders his servants to take care of Telemachus's horses and feed them. And then, this really gets me, Menelaus's maid-servants wash Telemachus and his men and "anoint" them with oil! I mean* really. *Then they feed them, etc. All of this before they even find out who Telemachus is.*

It all reminded me of my mother and how she's always going on about ole Carl Ray being a guest in our house. Well, I sure feel like his maidservant, but I'll tell you one thing: I wouldn't wash and anoint him for all the money in the world.

More Odyssey: *Everyone at Menelaus's starts crying and weeping about Odysseus (because they still think he's dead), but then a goddess gives them some special wine that prevents people from crying! Imagine.*

I wish I had some of that wine for Mrs. Furtz.

But Odysseus isn't dead. He's being held captive by a nymph named Calypso who apparently adores Odysseus and doesn't want him to go back to Penelope. Meanwhile, all Penelope's suitors decide to ambush Telemachus when he returns.

Wednesday, July 4
The Fourth of July!

I practically forgot this was the Fourth of July! Dad was at the kitchen table in his grungy clothes, and I asked him what he was doing there, and he said, "I live here." Har har. Then he said, "I'll give you a hint: firecrackers." Har har. I got it.

We all went on a picnic today to Windy Rock, a park about ten miles from Easton. In this park is the actual Windy Rock—a huge boulder up on top of a cliff. Supposedly you can walk up there anytime and the air will be still and silent until you reach the rock, and then, whoooosh, the wind blows as fierce as can be just around the rock. Sure enough, every time we've been there, it has happened. Next to the rock is a plaque that explains the legend behind it.

According to this legend, there once was an Indian maiden who fell to her death on this very cliff. Her lover came to the rock, wailing and moaning, and then he stood on the rock, ready to jump over too, because his life was nothing without his maiden. But then the winds started to blow round and round the rock so that he was unable to jump. The legend says the winds blew for two weeks (he must have been starving by then), until he fell into a deep slumber. Then the winds "abated" and his friends lifted him off the rock and took him home. And now every time anyone approaches the rock, the winds begin again. I guess the winds think he's coming back.

I like legends like that.

So we had a picnic there. Maggie didn't come because she went to a party with Kenny (she's ungrounded now), but Carl Ray came along. He's like a shadow. Everywhere we go, he goes.

Most of the day Dennis, Doug, and I climbed trees and just messed around. We put Tommy up in this one tree with us, and he was having a great time pretending the limb was a horse. Mom and Dad stayed on the blanket, just lying there and talking. Carl Ray walked around a lot, but then he started chasing us through the trees and he was reallllll scary.

I was surprised he had the energy to run, but he started tearing around pretending he was some kind of monster and making these horrible noises, and at first we all thought it was funny to see him like that, but then he kept it up, and I have to admit even *I* was scared, because he would run at us making these horrible faces and these horrible noises and he would grab one of us and drag us off until the others would come and pull the captive one free.

After a while Tommy and Dougie started crying and we all ran back to where Mom and Dad were. Then Carl Ray came walking up looking like his usual pale, pitiful self, and Mom and Dad didn't believe us that he had been scaring the living daylights out of everyone.

He's a strange one sometimes, that Carl Ray.

When it got dark, we watched the fireworks. I used to think fireworks were so terrific, but this year they seemed a little disappointing. You wait and wait all day, and then there's about ten minutes of booms and splashes of light and that's it.

Dad made a speech (which he makes every year) about Independence and Freedom and all. We're all so used to his speech that we don't really listen, but Carl Ray was hanging on every word, and when Dad was done Carl Ray said, "Thank you."

Dad said, "For what?"

Carl Ray said, "What you said was real nice."

Carl Ray is just full of surprises.

Thursday, July 5

Today was interesting (for a change). Real interesting.

Ready, O Muse?

Little did I know when rosy-fingered Dawn (child of morning) crept over the horizon today that it would be such a good day. Where shall I begin, Muse?

The pool. I went by myself because Maggie took Tommy, Dennis, and Dougie to the movies. I was going to go with them, but it was one of those days with clear blue sky and a little breeze and one of those sparkling suns (my Muse isn't exactly warmed up yet). Too nice to be all stuffed into a movie theater.

Sure enough, Alex Cheevey was at the pool again, just as he said. He was all by himself (I guess those Murphys don't swim at all), so we had a great time.

First we practiced diving. We were giving each other numbers (you know, like 10, 9, 8, etc.) for the quality of our dives. Then we started goofing around and doing clown dives and acting stupid.

At the first break we talked about the *Odyssey* because Alex happened to mention that he was reading it too. That surprised me, because even if he *was* reading it, I didn't think he'd be the type to admit it. He's farther along than I am and he actually *likes* it. He says it gets a lot more interesting as you go. But he's really into this bit about Telemachus finding his father. And do you know what he told me? He said he's always suspected he's *adopted*. He said he doesn't look or act like either one of his parents.

But, but, but. When the next break was called, he said, "Hey, let's leave." Did you catch that? He said "Let's," as in "Let *us*"! He wanted me to leave *with* him.

Then he walked me *home*. He didn't hang around because he had to go to work. He works part-time for a landscaping company, mowing lawns and pulling weeds and trimming bushes. Anyway, he said he had to work all day on Friday and Saturday, but, but, but, Alex Cheevey actually asked me if I wanted to go swimming again on Sunday! I mean he didn't just say, "Are you going to be at the pool on Sunday?" He actually said, "Want to go swimming on Sunday?"

See the difference? I do. Sigh.

The other interesting thing that happened concerns Carl Ray. At dinner, in the midst of all the usual pass-the-potatoes chatter, Maggie says, "Oh, by the way, Carl Ray, you had a phone call today."

Everyone stopped chewing because no one could imagine *who* would call Carl Ray. He's received a whole lot of letters from Aunt Radene, but not one single phone call.

Maggie said, "I wrote down the message," and from the kitchen she retrieved a piece of paper that she didn't give to Carl Ray. You could tell she wanted everyone to hear this. "It was a lady . . ."

Everyone about choked.

". . . who is the secretary of a Mr. Biggers." She stopped to take a bite of her beans. She chewed awhile. Carl Ray had stopped eating.

"And this lady, this secretary of Mr. Biggers's, wanted to know if you could come in and see Mr. Biggers . . ." and she took another bite of beans and chewed awhile. Meanwhile, we're all waiting.

". . . at four o'clock tomorrow afternoon. Apparently . . ." and she reached over for the jug of milk and poured herself a glass, ". . . this Mr. Biggers is a lawyer."

Carl Ray's mouth dropped open, revealing some unchewed potatoes.

"So you have this appointment at four tomorrow afternoon, and if you can't make it, you're supposed to call back. The number's right here at the bottom," and she handed the paper to Dennis, who handed it to Dougie, who handed it to Carl Ray, who just stared at it.

Dad said, "Carl Ray, do you have any idea what this is about?"

Carl Ray said, "Nope."

Dad looked at Mom, so she said, "Have you ever met this Mr. Biggers?"

Carl Ray said, "Nope."

Mom looked at Dad, so he said, "Hmmm. Are you *sure* you have no idea what this is about?"

Carl Ray said, "Nope."

Dad said, "Does that mean . . ." but then he stopped.

So everyone went on eating, except for Carl Ray, who sat there staring at this piece of paper. He didn't finish his dinner, which is a real sign that something must be wrong, because we all know what a gigantic appetite Carl Ray has.

After dinner, I heard Dad asking Carl Ray a bunch more questions. He asked him if this had anything to do with a girl ("Nope") or if Carl Ray was in any kind of trouble ("Nope") or if he owed anyone any money ("Nope") or if he'd been in any fights ("Nope") or stolen anything ("Nope"). Finally, Dad said he would leave work early tomorrow and take Carl Ray over to Mr. Biggers's office if Carl Ray wanted him to. Carl Ray said, "Okay."

I wonder what Carl Ray did that he's not telling anyone.

Thrashing Odysseus

> *Book Five of the* Odyssey *is all about Odysseus trying to get away from Calypso and being thrashed about on his raft until the goddesses help him. Lord.*

I asked my mom tonight if I was adopted and she about died laughing. "Whatever made you ask that?" she said (when she finally stopped laughing about ten hours later). "No, you are not adopted."

I was a little disappointed when she said that, and then I got to thinking that maybe she wouldn't want to tell me the truth, so maybe I *am* adopted, but I'll never really know unless she plans to tell me the truth when I'm sixteen. Actually, I've often suspected that I *am* adopted. Maybe Alex and I have the same parents! Oh, well, maybe that wouldn't be so good after all.

Friday, July 6

Boy, the gods are sure intervening in Carl Ray's life! I swear, Athene must have come down and taken pity on the poor creature. But before I tell about Carl Ray, I'll tell about Beth Ann as ole black-fingered night (grandfather of day) (har har har) (thanks, O Muse) creeps over the sky.

I took Tommy and Dougie for a walk today and we stopped at Beth Ann's. Even though she didn't seem real thrilled to see two little kids with me, she gave them some Coke and potato chips and we all went out into her backyard. While Tommy and Dougie climbed the apple tree, she and I actually talked for a change. I mean, it's *been* a while.

When I asked her about Derek, she acted as if they had been married for about a hundred years. She was so matter-of-fact about it all.

"Oh yes," she said, "we're still going out. He's over here all the time. My parents are VERY fond of him. Have you ever smelled Canoe? That's the kind of aftershave he wears. It's DI-VIIIIINE." *(There she goes again.)* "Judy says that's what all the college guys wear. I'm going to buy him some more for his birthday—that's next week. We're going out to dinner first—on his birthday, that is—and then back to his house for a little get-together" *(get-together??)* "with his parents and grandparents. They're such a nice family. I think I've met just about everyone in his family: his parents—they asked me to call them Betty and Bill—his brother, Gregory, of course—that's Judy's boyfriend—his grandparents—they asked me to call them Nonna and Poppa—his aunt Jean and uncle Roy; his aunt Catherine and uncle Bob. I think that's about it. Oh, and his best friend, whose name is Jerry—and Jerry's girlfriend, Molly. We've doubled with them a few times. Not too many times though, because Derek doesn't really like Molly. She talks so much."

Molly talks so much??? Have you ever heard anyone go on like Beth Ann does? How does she think of all those things to say? I am interested in what Beth Ann does, but really, should I be expected to care what Derek's grandparents want her to call them? Or what Derek's best friend's girlfriend's name is???

But I did pretend to be interested. You have to suffer through a few dozen of those things with Beth Ann in the hopes that she'll finally get to something meaty. I had to prompt her a little.

"So," I tried, "what do you and Derek *do* when you go out?"

"Oh, lots of things. We go to the movies and sometimes for a hamburger and—"

"You already told me all that. I meant what do you *do*, like, *after*ward?"

She gave me one of her funny smiles that meant "Oh, *I* get it," and then she looked around to see if Dougie and Tommy were near enough to hear. They weren't. She said, "Well—it *is* sort of personal. . . ."

"Beth Ann Bartels," I said, "I am your best friend, or at least I thought I was, and if you can't tell me . . ." I put on this real hurt look.

"Well—it's just that Derek wouldn't like it if I talked about Us like that," and she glanced at me, but I was still doing my hurt look, so she said, "but I know I can trust you."

"Well, I *hope* so!"

"Okay, then, but promise . . ."

"I *promise*! Geez, what do I have to do, swear on a Bible?"

"Okay, okay, don't get upset. Let's see. We *talk* a lot."

I rolled my eyes.

"Well, we *do*. He's a very interesting person, you know. He tells me all kinds of things, like about . . ."

"Beth Ann!"

"Right. You don't want to know about our conversations—you just want to know all the sordid details."

If anyone else had said this, I probably would have been mad, but she was being *so* ridiculous and of *course*

I wanted to know all the "sordid" details, so I just fell over laughing and then she fell over laughing and we were finally getting back to being good friends. Or so I thought.

Then I told her how much it had been bothering me that she hardly ever talked to me anymore and then when she did, all she could do was moon over Derek and talk like Megan and Christy: "di-viiiiine" and "truly wonderful" and all that. It felt good to tell her, and fortunately she didn't even seem to mind. She just laughed about it and said she was sorry and that she hadn't meant to sound so drippy and all.

But then I really blew it. I don't know what came over my brain, but I guess I thought I could go on being one hundred percent honest, and I said, "Well, maybe I was a little jealous. Maybe I was. When Maggie told me that she saw you and Derek at the party and that you were hanging all over him and that he was sort of a j—" All of a sudden I could tell by the look on her face that I had gone too far.

Boy, did she get mad! She straightened out her little mouth so fast into this flat little line and scrunched up her eyes and jumped up and said, "God, Mary Lou! Who do you think you are, anyway?!"

I started to apologize, but she wouldn't let me talk at all.

“I was NOT hanging all over Derek—believe me, I don’t have to do that. And Derek is NOT a jerk—don’t shake your head, I know that’s what you were going to say. You make me sick, and we’re NOT best friends, and you can take your little brat brothers and get out of my yard!” And she ran into the house and slammed the screen door and then slammed the other door and I heard the locks click.

Beth Ann is so darn touchy. Who does she think *she* is, anyway? It makes me mad just thinking about it now. I hate when someone yells at you and doesn’t even give you a chance to talk. I really hate that.

Grrrr.

So. Now about Carl Ray.

I just don’t believe this and apparently Dad doesn’t either, because when he got back from taking Carl Ray to see Mr. Biggers, he was shaking his head back and forth, and Carl Ray was looking sort of stunned. Everybody started jumping all over saying, “What happened? What did Mr. Biggers want? What did he say?” and Dennis said, “Is Carl Ray going to jail?” and Tommy started crying because I think he actually *likes* Carl Ray and he started screaming, “No jail! No jail!” and finally Dad got everybody quiet and made us sit down to dinner before he would tell us anything.

Here’s what happened: Mr. Biggers told Carl Ray

that someone wanted to give Carl Ray some money!!! Mr. Biggers "was not at liberty to divulge" the name of this person who is throwing his money away.

This sounds just like *Great Expectations*, if you ask me. *Great Expectations* is a terrific book. It's about a poor little boy who inherits some money and he thinks it's from this weird rich lady who sits around in this cobwebby room all day, but it turns out that the money is from some spooky convict who the boy gave some bread to when the boy was little.

But back to Carl Ray. We all just about keeled over when we heard about Mr. Biggers telling Carl Ray someone wanted to give him some money. It was chaos in our house because everybody started asking Carl Ray a million questions.

MAGGIE: Gosh, Carl Ray, who could the person be?
DENNIS: How much? How much did you get?
ME: Who is the person??
DOUGIE: Is it a lot of money?
TOMMY: No jail?
MAGGIE: Who do you think it could be?
ME: Yeah, who *is* it?
DENNIS: How much money is he giving you?
DOUGIE: Is he a millionaire?
TOMMY: No jail?

And on and on. Ole Carl Ray hardly had a chance to get a word in, and finally Dad yelled, "QUIET! WILL YOU ALL JUST BE QUIET?"

And when we finally all shut up, Dad said, "Carl Ray does not know who the person is. We've been through this already. He asked Mr. Biggers to tell him the name, but Mr. Biggers can't do that. Apparently whoever is giving Carl Ray this money wants to remain anonymous."

Mom said, "That's very curious, isn't it, Sam?"

Dad just nodded.

"Boy," Dennis said, "how lucky can a guy get? I wish this person would give *me* some money."

And Dougie said, "How much, Carl Ray?"

And Dad said, "Carl Ray, you don't have to tell them if you don't want to. It's none of their business."

Boy, here we are providing a hotel for the ole prince and Dad doesn't think it's any of our business?

But Carl Ray just shrugged and said, "I don't care if they know."

And Dennis said, "How much?"

And Carl Ray said to Dad, "You tell 'em. I forget." He for*gets*? Lord.

DAD: He gets five thousand dollars right now . . .
DENNIS: God!
MOM: Don't say "God!"

DOUGIE: GEEZ!!

MAGGIE: Wow.

ME: Lord.

TOMMY: No jail?

DAD: . . . and the rest of the money . . .

DOUGIE: There's *more*?

DENNIS: God!

MOM: Don't say "God!"

DAD: The rest of the money is being put in a trust fund to provide for Carl Ray's college education.

DENNIS: What college?

DOUGIE: What college?

MAGGIE: I didn't know you wanted to go to college, Carl Ray.

(I have to admit I was thinking "What college?" myself.)

MOM: Oh, be quiet all of you. Give Carl Ray a chance to think, will you?

ME: Well, *did* you want to go to college, Carl Ray?

(Carl Ray just shrugged.)

DENNIS: What if he doesn't *want* to go to college?

DOUGIE: Yeah, can he use that money for something

else? Like a television or something?

DAD: No. It's only for college. That's a condition on the rest of the money. If Carl Ray doesn't want to go to college, the money goes somewhere else, I guess.

DENNIS: Where does it go?

DOUGIE: Could I have it?

DAD: I don't know where it goes. No, you can't have it. It's all rather mysterious, if you ask me. All I know is what Mr. Biggers told us, and I don't want ANY of you repeating this to anyone. It is NO ONE's business but Carl Ray's, and Mr. Biggers asked that we keep this within the family.

Well, everyone was so excited. All of us kids spent the whole rest of the evening deciding what we would do if we got five thousand dollars and also we kept trying to guess who gave Carl Ray the money. We decided it was either some weird old lady who got Carl Ray mixed up with someone else, or maybe it was some long-lost uncle who had so much money he didn't know what to do with it. Or maybe it was some strange old convict who Carl Ray met just once and maybe Carl Ray gave him some bread or something. You just never know about these things.

Carl Ray doesn't seem too excited, but he does seem worried. I can't imagine why, unless he thinks maybe it's a mistake and tomorrow Mr. Biggers will call and say the person changed his mind or got the wrong Carl Ray or something.

Naked Odysseus

Book Six of the Odyssey *is all about some ladies doing their laundry and Odysseus coming naked out of the sea and since he's been twenty days thrashing about in the water, he looks pretty awful, but he's real polite and coherent and asks them to move away while he washes because he's ashamed of being naked. Then, with a little help and anointing from Athene, he emerges looking terrific, like a god and all. As usual, even though he's a total stranger, they all welcome him and give him clothes and everything.*

Saturday, July 7

Everyone's still asking Carl Ray a million questions about the money and wondering who gave it to him, and he's still walking around looking shocked, although I did see him looking through the Sears catalogue. Maybe he's trying to decide what to buy first.

Mom got real mad at all of us today. She sent Dennis and Dougie to their room (she hardly ever does that) because they kept badgering Carl Ray, telling him they sure did wish they could have a new bicycle (that was Dougie) and a little television (Dennis) and all kinds of other stuff: toys, baseball bats, ice skates, roller skates, stilts, water skis (we don't even have a boat) and on and on.

Mom got mad at Maggie because she just happened to mention to Carl Ray that there was a beee-yooo-teee-ful coat at the May Company that she was absolutely in love with. She got mad at Tommy because he badgered her all day about Carl Ray going to jail. She got mad at me because I wrote "Mary Lou's favorite wish" on a picture of a desk and taped it on the wall outside Carl Ray's bedroom. Mom said, "You can be very insensitive, Mary Lou."

Me? Insensitive?

Sunday, July 8

I just don't even know where to start. Maybe at the pool. I went to the pool today (after Carl Ray the Prince finally got out of bed so I could clean up that room—I still have to vacuum in there, which does not seem fair since Carl

Ray's *only* chore so far is to make up his stupid bed). Alex asked me if I wanted to go swimming today, remember? Sure enough, Alex was there.

It was all cloudy and cool though, so after about an hour we decided (it was Alex's idea) to go somewhere else. It sure seemed like something was bothering him, and I thought, Well, maybe he was sorry he asked me to meet him there, and maybe he was trying to think of a way to get rid of me. We went to this little park near the pool and sat on a picnic table. For a while we just read all the names carved into the table, and I was about to say that I had to go home (just in case he did want to get rid of me, I thought I'd better make it sound like I was ready to go anyway), when he said, "I got the strangest phone message the other day."

"What message?"

"Some girl called and said to my mother, 'Tell Alex I love him.'" Then he looked at me as if he was waiting for me to confess.

Boy was I *mad*. I was mad because, first of all, it wasn't ME who called, but Alex thought it was, and second of all, I was wondering who in the heck DID call. Grrrr. But before I could say anything, Alex looks up because this girl is walking toward us. She's smiling and waving her arm like crazy, and when she gets pretty close, she says, "Hiiiiiii! Hiiiiiii there!"

It was Christy, from school. I thought I was going to have a heart attack.

She started drooling all over Alex. "Hiiiii, Alex. Oh hi, Mary Lou. Whatever are you doing over here, Alex? I'm here with my cousin. Did you ever meet my cousin Carol? She's up there," and she pointed toward the pool and batted her eyelashes at Alex and wiggled her shoulders and SAT DOWN next to Alex on the picnic table.

"Hi," said Alex.

I didn't say one word.

"So, what are you *doing* over here, Alex? Huh? Huh?"

"Nothing."

"*Nothing?* So why are you over *here* doing nothing? You live way over in *Norton*!!" She turned to me and said, "Have you ever seen Alex's house? *I* have. I just *love* your mom, Alex. She's so *sweet*. I can't believe you're way over here in *Easton*. Don't you go swimming in *Norton*, huh Alex, huh?"

On and on and on she went, babbling away like that, asking about a million questions and never giving Alex a chance to answer anything. I didn't think she was *ever* going to leave. I started counting the leaves on this tree next to the table, just to keep from punching her one. I got up to 367 before she finally said, "So hey, Alex, why don't you come up and go swimming with me and my cousin? Oh, you too, Mary Lou. Come on, Alex, won't you?" Wiggle wiggle. Smile smile.

And then Alex said, "Can't. Have to go home."

So she made this little pouty mouth and said, "Well, Carol's waiting for me. I'll let you off this time, Alex. . . ." Wiggle wiggle. Smile smile. And, at last, she got up and wiggled away.

We sat there for a few minutes. Then I said, "Do you really have to go home now?"

And he said, "Nope."

Then I said, "I think I just figured out who left you that phone message."

He looked a little disappointed. "Huh?"

"Well, it wasn't *me*!" And I gave a meaningful look in Christy's direction. She was still wiggling off in the distance.

"Ahhh," he said.

And then you would not believe what he did next.

He put his hand on top of mine. At first I didn't know if it was an accident or on purpose and I was wondering if I should move my hand. But he pressed his down a little bit, so I figured it was on purpose. Then I started wondering if I should turn my hand *over*—then he could hold it—but what if he didn't *want* to hold it? How am I supposed to know what he's *thinking*? I decided to leave my hand the way it was. If he wanted to turn it over, he could do that himself.

When I think about it right now, I could just swoon away.

And then do you know what he said? He said, "I like you, Mary Lou Finney."

And I just sat there like some idiot. I just sat there staring at him. He looked so different all of a sudden. He looked like Odysseus probably did when he cleaned himself up and anointed himself after being in the ocean for three weeks. All the girls standing around Odysseus about fell over from his beauty. They thought he was some kind of a god. And that's what Alex looked like to me. His skin was so pink and healthy-looking and his hair was all clean and shiny and he smelled just like soap.

Well, that sounds ridiculous, I know. Almost as bad as Beth Ann mooning over Derek-the-Di-viiiiine.

Anyway, then Alex got up and he said, "I'll walk you home," and he TOOK MY HAND (which turned over automatically, I think) and we walked home, and I still couldn't talk at all, and just before we got to the corner of my street I pretended I had to scratch my ankle so I could let go of his hand because even though I really liked holding his hand, I would have died if anyone in my family saw that. And at the corner of my street, he said, "Well, I guess I'll go on home," and I said, " 'Bye," and he said, " 'Bye," and then he started walking away and all of a sudden I said, "Oh, wait!" and he turned around and smiled and walked back, and he said, "I'll call you."

And I truly thought I was sitting on Mount Olympus.

And I know this is boring you to death, whoever you are, and I know I will never ever be able to turn this in to any English teacher after saying all this mush.

But . . .

I can hardly stand it. . . .

Monday, July 9

I don't even want to write about Carl Ray and stuff.

Mary Lou Cheevey. Mrs. Alex Cheevey. Mary Lou and Alex. Mary Lou Finney and Alex Cheevey.

I can hardly breathe.

I didn't even go out of the house today in case Alex called—which he didn't and I think I will probably die if he doesn't.

Oh, God! What am I saying? I hate it when girls moon over boys. I refuse to moon over Alex Cheevey.

But Lord! All day long I kept coming up to my room and lying on my bed so I could remember exactly what happened yesterday and exactly what it felt like holding his hand, and really, if someone else said this to me I would throw up.

I can't write any more. I just want to think about it.

I'll write about Carl Ray and stuff tomorrow.

Tuesday, July 10

I still can't write. I am hopeless. Alex called today and he came over. I am on Mount Olympus. I'll write about everything tomorrow. I promise.

Wednesday, July 11

Alex had to work all day and couldn't come over, but he did call and I still am worthless and so I'll write tomorrow but I am soooooo happeeeeee I can hardly stand it. I just want to think about it.

Thursday, July 12

Well, I still am worthless, but I feel terrible for not keeping track of everything and I *will* catch up right now.

I think all of a sudden I realize why Beth Ann wouldn't tell me about Derek and why she's soooo strange these days. Because I'm acting just as weird as she is, I swear. I'm turning into a real lunatic. All over a boy.

I cannot believe it. I am going to try not to act like this. But I see why Beth Ann didn't want to talk about Derek. You want to keep it floating around in your mind and keep it secret, because there is no way you can explain it to anyone without sounding like a complete idiot.

But I am really going to try. I am going to be reasonable about this. And so first I will talk about everything else. (But God! I LOVE ALEX CHEEVEY!!!!!!)

It's funny, but when you don't write things down every day, you forget when things happened.

First, Carl Ray. He bought a car! I didn't even know he knew how to drive. He doesn't have it yet (the car)—it's supposed to be ready tomorrow. He won't even tell us what kind it is or anything. Maybe he wants it to be a big surprise. Or maybe he *forgot* what kind of car he bought.

Just about everybody is still hinting like mad for Carl Ray to buy them things, only they don't hint when Mom is around because she gets so mad. I even heard Dad hinting. He was saying how the lawn mower is a piece of junk and he wishes he had a new one and he even looked through the Sears catalogue (coincidentally when Carl Ray was sitting there watching TV) and kept saying things like, "Oh, *here's* a nice one. Too much money, though. Oh well."

Mom keeps asking Carl Ray if he has written to his parents yet, to tell them about the money, and Carl Ray keeps saying, "Nope." That does seem a little strange—that he hasn't told his own parents—don't you think? Tonight, Mom said, "Carl Ray, if you don't write them pretty soon, *I* will," and Carl Ray looked so mournful and sad that she turned to my dad, and he said, "Don't look at *me*."

One other thing about Carl Ray, while I am on the subject. He's been watering the Furtzes' lawn without anybody asking him to or without getting any "gold" for it. What do you think of that?

Now I will talk about the truly wonderful and di-viiiiine Alex Cheevey.

He came over TO MY HOUSE on Tuesday. I was upstairs when I heard Dennis shouting, "MARY LOUUU, MARY LOUUU, THERE'S A BOY AT THE DOOR. MARY LOUUU, MARY LOUUU, THERE'S A BOY HERE FOR YOUUU." Honestly. It was embarrassing. He made it sound like it was the strangest thing in the world for a boy to be here for me.

And when I came downstairs, there was Dougie standing with his nose pressed against the screen staring at Alex and there was Tommy right next to him, without any pants on at all.

Alex waited on the porch while I begged and pleaded with Maggie to watch Tommy and the others while Alex and I went out for a few hours. She asked me about a thousand questions ("Well, who IS this boy?"—"Oh, is this the Alex I met?"—"Don't you want me to say hello?"—"Where are you going?"—and on and on in this singsong voice) but finally she agreed, if I would give her this red scarf I have. I gave it to her.

When I escaped from the madhouse, Alex and I walked to the end of our street and then I decided to show him the big tree over in the field, the one where Dennis, Dougie, and I used to go all the time, the one that looks like a fort underneath. So we walked over there and went in under the branches and sat down and talked.

I can't even remember half of what we talked about. Part of the problem is I'm not sure I was always paying attention, because when I am with Alex my brain is like mush and mostly I am just looking at him and feeling as if my muscles are melting and my blood is filled with millions of little bubbles all fizzing around.

So we held hands right there under the tree. It was very romantic. And in the middle of that, do you know what he told me?

He said that he made up the Murphys—they don't exist! All those times he was over on our street and up at the pool, it was just because of ME!!!!! He was coming over to see me, but he didn't have the nerve to say so because he thought I would tell him to jump in the lake or something.

Can you imagine that?

Well, I love Alex Cheevey. I really do.

Good night.

Friday, July 13

Egad, Friday the thirteenth. Well, it wasn't unlucky for me, at least. In fact, it was a pretty lucky day for everybody I know except Beth Ann. But I'll explain that in a minute.

Carl Ray came home in his car today. I have to admit, it's a pretty cute thing. A little black Ford with red (red!!! Carl Ray???) seats. He's so proud of it, he almost died from grinning so much. He made us all come outside and look at it and sit in it, and after dinner he actually took me, Dennis, and Dougie for a ride in it to the Tast-ee Freeze (and he even bought us ice cream), and then when we got home, he spent about two hours polishing it, even though it was as clean as can be. Boy, is he happy.

Except for the ice cream, he still hasn't bought anyone anything, but the Sears catalogue is about to fall apart from so many people looking through it.

Now, Alex. He didn't have to be at work until four o'clock today, so we went to the pool early and then, on the way home, just as we were turning the corner of my street, who should we bump into but Beth Ann. Boy, was she surprised to see Alex Cheevey, the Truly Wonderful and Divine, holding my hand!

She stood there with her mouth gaping open. You could see all her fillings. Boy, did she look terrible. Her eyes were all puffy and red and she looked like a complete wreck. She said, "I need to talk to you, Mary Lou," and she kept looking at me and then Alex and then me and then Alex, as if her head was on a bouncy spring and she couldn't control it. You know those dogs people put on the back ledges of their cars? Like that.

Alex said he had to go, so off he went. (Sigh.)

I was pretty surprised that Beth Ann wanted to talk to me. I seemed to recall that the last time I saw her, she told me that I made her sick and we weren't best friends anymore. But she seems to have forgotten that.

Well! To make a very, very, very, very long story short, she and Derek broke up. Apparently, Derek has been messing around with someone else, and the way Beth Ann found out about it was that she went to the store with her sister Judy, and when they came out to the parking lot they saw Derek-the-Di-viiiiine walking with some girl and he had his arm around her!

And do you know what Beth Ann did? She went right up to ole Derek and this girl and asked him what he was doing and he looked at her like she was a stranger. He called her today and said that maybe they should both see other people for a while.

God.

It's funny, but if this had happened a week ago, I probably would have been happy in a very mean way. But now I feel sorry for Beth Ann, even if she has been acting like a real snot. I mean she was *really* upset, sobbing and all. I was afraid she was going to go completely hysterical.

The only thing was she didn't even ask me about Alex, and I have to admit that even though I wasn't ready to tell her any *details* or anything, I did sort of want to brag about him a little. But I could tell she didn't exactly want to hear how happy I was and how wonderful Alex was when she was suffering this enormous tragedy.

I read Books Seven and Eight of the *Odyssey* but I can't remember any of it. I haven't been able to concentrate too well lately. I keep thinking about Alex right in the middle of reading.

Saturday, July 14

Well, this evening was almost a complete disaster.

Alex came over at six thirty. We were going to walk to the movies. But first he had to come in and my parents had to do their how-very-nice-to-meet-you routine and check him out and all. They made such a fuss that it was embarrassing. You could tell that they thought he was an okay kind of guy, and I have to admit that if I was a parent, I would think so too. He just looks so *clean* and all. He didn't talk much, just "hello" and "yes" and stuff, but I think they liked that about him.

Anyway, there they were going on and on about how nice it was to meet Alex and where were we going and when would we be back, and in the middle of all this, there sits Carl Ray watching TV, and Maggie walks through in her curlers and bathrobe, and Dennis and Dougie are gaping over the stairway, and Tommy is putting his finger in his nose. Honestly. What is Alex going to think?

I couldn't *wait* to get out of there.

But just as soon as we walked out the front door and I was about to breathe an enormous sigh of relief, who comes following us out but Carl Ray, the Shadow. He says, "Want a ride?"

Alex was surprised because he's not as used to Carl Ray sneaking up on people as I am, and I was surprised because I couldn't believe Carl Ray was actually offering to do us a favor. But I figured he just wanted to show off his car and it would be nice to have a ride. So we said sure.

It was kind of strange, Alex and I riding in the backseat and Carl Ray driving us like our chauffeur.

Alex was sitting way over near his door, and I was way over near mine. Carl Ray kept looking at us in his rear-view mirror.

So we get to the movie theater and I'm wondering why Carl Ray is pulling around the back instead of dropping us in front, but I didn't say anything. And I did think it was kind of funny when he pulled into a parking space. And I started to get a little uneasy when we got out and he got out too.

Sure enough, ole Carl Ray drops the big bomb: "I think I'll come too."

Alex gave me this horrified look and I gave Alex a horrified look. I said to Carl Ray, "You'll come *too*?"

And he said, "Yup. Might as well. Long as I'm here."

I wonder if my parents paid Carl Ray to do this.

He stood with us in line and bought his ticket, and stood in line with us while we bought popcorn, and the whole time I was sweating like crazy trying to think how in the world we could get *rid* of him and I couldn't even say anything to Alex because Carl Ray was right there, the Shadow, the whole time.

I thought I was going to die.

He followed us to our seats and sat right next to me! I was in between Carl Ray and Alex. I gave Alex one of those I-don't-believe-this-is-happening looks and then I gave him a how-in-the-world-are-we-going-to-ditch-him?

look and he gave me one of those oh-well-what-can-we-do? looks and then the movie started.

I won't go into all the details, like how Carl Ray watched every move Alex made and every time Alex moved his arm, Carl Ray turned and looked at his arm like it was a snake or something. I won't go into that.

I will just say that I was a complete wreck and I couldn't wait to get out of there.

But Alex and I must have both been thinking the same thing, because when it was finally over and we got outside and started walking to the car, Alex said, "Hey, Mary Lou, why don't we walk home?"

I said, maybe a little too quickly, "Oh, great idea! It's sooooo nice out."

Alex said to Carl Ray, "Thanks a lot for the ride! You don't mind if we walk home, do you?"

For the eternity of about five seconds, I thought Carl Ray was going to find some way to get us in his car, but all he did was give us this little sad look and say, "Naw. Go ahead."

I almost felt sorry for him, but then I figured we were entitled to a *little* privacy, weren't we? Do you think Carl Ray is lonely?

Alex and I had the greatest time walking home. We were both in such a good mood. The closer we got to my house, the slower we walked. Then I started getting a little nervous, thinking he might try and kiss me or something. I don't know the first thing about it. I need some practice. But he didn't do anything like that.

Sunday, July 15

I wish this summer could go on and on and on, and I wish I could always be this happy. It seems that whenever you are sad or just normal, you're always wishing you were happy, but when you're happy, you start worrying about when all this happiness is going to end. At least that's the way I am. Already, I'm worrying that I'm too happy, and I'm either going to have to pay for this or it's all going to end real soon.

It reminds me of the wheel of fortune that Mrs. Zollar talked about. She said that Shakespeare and all his buddies believed in the wheel of fortune, that your luck kind of went round and round, and when you (or your luck) were at the top, everything would go right. But that it was inevitable that the wheel had to keep spinning, and sooner or later, you'd be at the bottom of the wheel, when everything would go badly. The only thing that kept people from jumping off cliffs when they were at the bottom of the wheel was knowing that sooner or later they would be at the top again.

I feel as if the gods are going to spin my wheel any minute. Oh, pleeease, let me stay where I am for a while!

I also wish everyone's wheel was at the top at the same time. Beth Ann, for instance, is at the bottom of her wheel and she's driving me crazy. She must have called me ten times today to tell me about Derek. First she said that he was a complete creep and she never wanted to see him again and she cried. Then she called back and said that she loved him sooooo much and maybe she should call him and tell him how much she missed him, and she cried. Then she called back and said she figured out why he was doing this: to make her jealous because he liked her so much, and she cried. Get the picture?

And, of course, she never once gave me a chance to say one word about Alex.

Alex, by the way, called at lunchtime (I don't know how he was able to get through, what with Beth Ann calling all the time) to say he couldn't come over today because he had to go to his grandmother's house with his parents. It was his grandmother's birthday and a whole bunch of relatives would be there.

Since I didn't have too much to do today and since it was raining like crazy, I stayed home and read some more of the *Odyssey*. I think I'm getting to the good parts.

Lotus-Eaters and Cyclopes

In Book Nine, Odysseus starts telling about all these great adventures he's had. There were two I really liked.

One was about lotus-eaters, people who eat flowers. When Odysseus and his men visited them, his men ate a bunch of lotus flowers and it made them forget all about their home and their loved ones and they wanted to stay with the lotus-eaters forever. (I wonder if that's what happened to ole Derek!!??) But Odysseus forces them back on their ship and he ties them to some benches and they leave. (They're trying to get home after they've sacked all these cities.)

Then they come to the land of the Cyclopes, a weird group who live in caves and don't have any laws. Odysseus and some of his men go up to the cave of this horrible one-eyed monster Cyclops, and pretty soon this Cyclops starts smashing a couple of the men on the ground and tears out their arms and legs and stuff and eats them. (Ugh.) That's for supper. He does it again for breakfast. Finally, Odysseus (who, if you ask me, brags a little too much about his cleverness) comes up with this great plan. He tells the monster his name is "Noman," and then he gets the monster drunk and pokes his eye out with this huge burning club. Homer really gets into all the gory details too, about the eye bubbling and hissing and all. It's a little too much for me.

But the best part is when this monster's friends all come and start calling to him, asking why he is screaming and stuff. And he says that "Noman" (no man, get it?) is killing him, and since his friends think that no man is killing him, they go away. Anyway, they all (or at least the ones who haven't been eaten) finally do escape through Odysseus's plan (he's real proud of it) of tying them underneath some sheep and goats who are in the cave and will be let out in the morning. It's a little hard to imagine.

The only thing I don't like about Odysseus is that he brags so much about how clever he is and how many cities he sacked and how many people he killed. I think he'd be put in jail if he were alive today.

Monday, July 16

Another rainy, cloudy day.

Alex called, but he couldn't come over because he's got the flu. I bet he caught it at his grandmother's birthday party. He said the party was a real bore except for the part when she opened the present from Alex's grandfather (her husband). It was a black negligee!! Imagine.

Not a real exciting day here. Mom left us all a note today saying we had to wash all the windows in the whole entire house. We called her at work to tell her it was raining, but she said we had to do the insides anyway. The worst thing is, you can't really SEE how much work we did, because the windows are still all dirty on the outside. I hope it's still raining tomorrow. I don't think I could take another day of smelling that vinegar and toiling my arm off.

I miss Alex Cheevey. Sigh.

Beth Ann is still calling a million times a day. She has written and torn up about fifty letters to Derek. Her latest plan is to make Derek jealous, but she doesn't exactly know how she's going to do it.

She also told me something that really surprised me. Christy (from school) called her. They're not even friends or anything. Anyway, Christy was yakking away about a bunch of nonsense and she told Beth Ann some "secret" news that Beth Ann wasn't supposed to tell anyone. Beth Ann told me though. This secret news is that Christy, Megan, and a bunch of other goony girls like them have formed a club called GGP and they can't tell ANYONE what GGP stands for. And Christy told Beth Ann that Beth Ann was "under consideration" for membership in this stupid club.

That really made me mad.

First of all, why Beth Ann? Why not me? Not that I would join their stupid GGP anyway. They know Beth Ann and I are best friends. What are they trying to do, anyway? Beth Ann thinks they will probably call me too, but I can't believe it. I told Beth Ann that I didn't want to join their stupid GGP, and I asked Beth Ann if she was going to join if they asked her to, and she said she *didn't know.* As if maybe she *might.* I said, "Without me?" And she said, "Oh, I don't know!"

Mrs. Furtz came over after dinner tonight to ask my dad if he would kill a spider in her kitchen. I thought my dad would laugh at her, but he said, "Why, of course," and off he went and she waited here and when Dad came back, she started crying and saying how she was so pathetic and helpless and didn't think she could go on. Mom and Dad talked with her for about three hours in the kitchen, and they sent Maggie over to put her kids to bed. It was pretty sad. She looks horrible. You'd think the gods might have taken into account how much Mr. Furtz was needed at home.

Mom keeps asking Carl Ray when he is going to let his parents know about the money and the college education. Carl Ray has been saying, "Pretty soon," but tonight he said he thought he would surprise them. He wants to take a week off work and drive home to show them his new car. He hasn't asked his boss (the old Mr. Furtz's brother) yet, though.

I've decided not to read the *Odyssey* at night anymore. I had such awful dreams last night. Someone was chasing me with this enormous pointed stick, trying to poke my eye out, and I was almost trampled to death by a herd of goats. So I read some Robert Frost poems tonight. I won't write in red ink because I don't understand poetry very well.

Robert Frost doesn't seem to have a very big vocabulary. I bet he didn't do very well in English. But once you get used to his poems, they're okay. I've always liked that one about stopping by the woods on a snowy night. We've had to read it (and memorize it) just about every year in English. I swear, it's every English teacher's favorite poem.

Last year in English class we had a big fight over it, because Mrs. Zollar was talking about the symbolism in it and asking people what they thought the road and the woods symbolized. People were saying some pretty strange things. I could see how the woods could be death, but why would he think they were so beautiful? Then someone said, Well maybe the woods symbolized "fun"—like he wants to go have fun, but he can't because he has so many more miles to go. Well, that was stretching it, I thought, but it was possible. Then people got carried away and started saying maybe the woods represented ice cream or surfing and someone even said they symbolized sex and it was all getting out of control and finally Bonnie Argentini said that the whole thing was ridiculous and maybe Robert Frost just meant for the woods to be woods and it made her sick how everyone was always trying to say what the author meant when no one could possibly know. Then Billy Kroger told her to shut up, that she was too dense to see the "hidden meaning," and it all went to pot after that, with people shouting and stuff, and you could tell Mrs. Zollar was sorry she ever brought it up.

Mr. Furtz is in the woods, but I have miles to go before I sleep.

Tuesday, July 17

Oh groannn. Can't write. Have the flu.

Wednesday, July 18

Still feel lousy but at least have stopped throwing up. Talked to Alex. He's all better.

Thursday, July 19

I've recovered. Now Dennis and Dougie are sick.

I finally saw Alex again today, but I couldn't go anywhere with him because I had to help Maggie take care of Dennis and Dougie, who are throwing up all over the place. It's disgusting.

But Alex and I did get to be alone for about ten whole minutes. Sighhhhh. Here's what happened. We were sitting on the front porch, and he said, "I like it when you wear that pink shirt." (I was wearing a pink T-shirt.) I never thought boys noticed what girls wore. I thought I could wear a trash bag and no boy would ever know the difference. And *then* Alex reached over and touched the sleeve of my shirt, as if he was checking out its pinkness or something. Well, when he touched that sleeve, I thought, Oh boy, this is it, he's going to kiss me now. I could just feel it coming. I was dissolving into a blithering idiot.

But then Tommy started banging on the door behind us, and Alex moved his hand (alas, alas!), and Maggie said I had to go in, and I looked at Alex and he looked at me, and I said, "I like it when you wear that blue shirt" (he was wearing his blue T-shirt), and he smiled.

Ohhhhh. Is this disgusting or what? What's the

matter with me? Do you think he was going to kiss me? I wish there was a manual for this sort of thing, something that would tell you about holding hands and kissing. When should this happen? How many days should you hold hands before you kiss? Sometimes I just can't wait for that kiss, but sometimes I think, *Ugh! Please don't!* I wish I'd make up my mind. I wonder if Alex thinks the same things. Do boys actually think about this mushy stuff? Or do they just automatically know what to do?

We're going to the movies again tomorrow. Only this time we will INSIST on walking and NOT TELL Carl Ray where we are going!

Beth Ann has finally decided to take some action in her battle against Derek (who is now referred to as "that jerk"). She has read to me three drafts of the letter she is sending tomorrow. It's all about how she loved him and trusted him and how he betrayed her and he could at least have the common decency to give her an explanation. She asked me if I thought she should send it and I said that I thought she should just forget him and NOT send it, but she decided to send it anyway. So much for my good advice.

The other thing she is thinking of doing is REVOLTING and shows you just how much this whole thing with Derek has affected her brain. She wanted to know, get this, if I thought CARL RAY liked her and if he maybe would ask her out if I suggested it!!!!!! I thought she was kidding, but she sure wasn't. I said, "What for???" He's *four* years older than Beth Ann, though I guess he doesn't act it.

And she said, "Well, he's kind of cute."

And I said, *"Carl Ray?"* I really could not believe it. Carl Ray, cute? The same Carl Ray who sneaks around here and never makes up his stupid bed? That Carl Ray???

I told her I didn't want any part of it, but she said that she only wanted to make Derek jealous, and if Carl Ray would ask her out, she would get him to take her to all the places she and Derek used to go so that maybe she would run into him and his new girlfriend, and that maybe if Derek saw her with someone else he would realize how much he missed her, and on and on.

Now, that's a *desperate* mind at work, if you ask me.

I didn't agree to anything yet. I said I had to think about it.

Honestly.

Friday, July 20

I have about a million things to say, but my brain is too mushy from being with Alex, so they will all have to wait for tomorrow. I do love Alex Cheevey!!!!

Saturday, July 21

Saw Alex again, so cannot think.

A lot is happening, though, so I promise to catch up tomorrow.

Sunday, July 22

There are wicked thunderstorms outside right now. The wind is bashing the trees around and the trash cans are rolling down the driveway.

Mrs. Zollar said that Shakespeare and his buddies thought that if there was a storm, it was because the universe was out of whack somewhere. And the Greeks believed storms were caused by gods who were mad at someone. Actually, I think it's just a storm.

Didn't see Alex today (he had to go to his grandmother's again), so I can at least think tonight. I'll wait and tell about Alex at the end so I don't start getting all mushy before I remember everything else.

The most disgusting news is that Beth Ann went out with Carl Ray.

She called me on Friday morning to say that she had finally mailed a letter to "the jerk" (alias Derek-the-Divine).

Beth Ann wrote this very gushy letter (she read a copy of it to me—she kept a *copy*!) to Derek all about how much she loved him and how maybe they *should* both see other people, because that way they would be able to know for sure if their hearts were telling the truth (how can hearts tell the truth?).

Then she asked me if I had hinted to Carl Ray about taking her out and I said no, I hadn't, so she made me go with her to the hardware store to see him. It went something like this:

(Scene: Two girls, Mary Lou and Beth Ann, enter hardware store. A seventeen-year-old gangly, pale, freckled boy with a tiny bird head and enormous hands and feet [Carl Ray] is straightening the display of insect repellents. He looks up, turns brilliant red, and then continues to straighten display.)

BETH ANN: *(whispering to Mary Lou)* Come on then. Say something to him.

MARY LOU: *(also whispering)* This is ridiculous.

(They walk up to Carl Ray. He's still straightening cans.)

MARY LOU: So hi there, Carl Ray.

CARL RAY: Hi.

MARY LOU: So. You know Beth Ann here, don't you?

CARL RAY: *(still straightening cans)* Unnh.

BETH ANN: *(in her Marilyn Monroe voice)* Hellooooo, Carl Ray. I haven't seen you in ages.

(Carl Ray looks up. He's not completely stupid.)

CARL RAY: Enh.

MARY LOU: So whatcha doin', Carl Ray?

CARL RAY: Workin'.

MARY LOU: Ah.

BETH ANN: I bet you have a lot of responsibility here.

CARL RAY: What's your name again?

BETH ANN: Beth Ann. Beth Ann Bartels. B-A-R-T-E-L-S. I live over at six-two-two Holmden Road. Right around the corner from Mary Lou.

MARY LOU: *(aside to Beth Ann)* Why don't you give him your phone number or something?

BETH ANN: *(aside to Mary Lou)* Oh, shut up.

CARL RAY: *(to Mary Lou)* You want something?

MARY LOU: Huh?

CARL RAY: From the store?

MARY LOU: Oh. Uh—

BETH ANN: No, we don't want anything. We just came in to see you.

CARL RAY: Huh?

BETH ANN: Oh, we were just in the neighborhood, and I said to Mary Lou, why don't we go in and see your cousin, since we're right here, because, I said, I haven't seen your cousin in *ages* and I wonder how he's doing. So Mary Lou said okay, although she can't stay long because she has to go home to get ready for her *date* with Alex. They're going to the *movies*. They're going to see that real good movie about the guy who inherits his father's ranch and there's this girl—well, actually, I don't know too much about it because *I* haven't seen it yet, but I hear it's a romance, sort of, but it has adventure too. And it's a little sad but also funny too. That's what I hear. Maybe Mary Lou will tell me all about it after she and Alex see it tonight. I guess I'll just stay home and read or something boring like that. Don't you hate these beautiful summer nights when all there is to do is sit home and *read*?

CARL RAY: What'd you say your name was again?

BETH ANN: Beth Ann Bartels. I live at—

MARY LOU: Excuse me, but I'm going to go over there and look at wallpaper paste. I'll be right over there if either of you needs me.

(Scene fades out.)

Well, she did it. She got him to ask her to the movies. Unbelievable. And her parents are *letting* her go. When I told my mother, she said, "Beth Ann? With Carl Ray? But he's seventeen years old! Whatever can her parents be *thinking*?"

Exactly.

But then Beth Ann wanted me and Alex to go with them! I really thought that was stretching friendship a bit far. I refused. So they went to the movie that *we* wanted to see (and which, by the way, Beth Ann has seen three times already), and we walked down to the Big Boy and had a hamburger and then we went to the park (by the pool) and sat on the picnic tables.

We held hands for twenty minutes (I had my watch on). I've been practicing kissing on one of Maggie's posters—there's one of a guy who has approximately life-size lips—just in case Alex decides to kiss me. Sometimes I think he's going to, but he gets all nervous and never does. I'm a little glad. I hope, when the time comes, I have a chance to brush my teeth first. I also hope that it doesn't taste like chicken.

On Saturday, Beth Ann called me to tell me how wonnnnderful Carl Ray is (Carl Ray? Wonnnnderful?) and that they were going out *again* that night. Unbelievable. She *loves* his car (maybe she's just after his money) and she thinks he's shy (well, that's true) and cute (pretty far-fetched, if you ask me) and *such* a gentleman (I think she's making this up) and sooooo interesting (absolutely a bald-faced lie).

She also said that she didn't think "the jerk" (Derek) got her letter yet (well, of *course* not, she just mailed it the day before), and, no, they hadn't run into "the jerk" at the movies (probably because she had made him take her to it three times already), but sooner or later she and Carl Ray (she's talking like she owns him now or something) were bound to run into the ole jerk.

Beth Ann also said that Christy had called her that morning (Saturday) and told her that the GGP (the secret club) was having a pajama party that night and only a few non-GGP girls were invited, and that these non-GGP girls were "under consideration for membership." They invited Beth Ann to the party, but she told Christy she couldn't go because she had a date with an older man (oh, brother). Beth Ann decided this was good strategy anyway, and it would make them even more anxious for her to join.

Then Beth Ann said that Christy asked her a million questions about me and Alex, but Beth Ann said she really didn't know too much about Alex because I don't tell her very much. As if she ever gives me a chance to get a word in.

Then Beth Ann said that Christy was probably going

to call me at any minute so I'd better get off the phone.

Christy didn't call.

The other news is that Carl Ray is going home next Friday. When I mentioned that to Beth Ann today, she about blew a gasket. You'd think they were married or something. She said, "Oh, how can he leave me *now*?" and "Why does he have to go on the *weekend*?" and all that kind of malarkey.

Wild Winds and Pig-Men

I read Book Ten of the Odyssey *yesterday afternoon. It was pretty good, but there are some very strange parts. For instance, King Aeolus lives on an island and he had six sons and six daughters and he made them* marry *each other (how* disgusting*), I guess because of the island and no other people being around. The King gives Odysseus a present. It's a bag of winds. Really, a bag full of crazy, wild winds, the kind that are blowing around outside right now. So Odysseus takes this weird present and off he goes, but when he falls asleep, his nosy men open the bag and the winds get out and there's this horrible storm and they get tossed around and are driven about eight million miles away from their home (they were almost home until this happened).*

Then they go to another island, where Circe lives, and she changes all the men (except Odysseus, who, of course, is too clever) into pigs (Homer really gets carried away sometimes). Circe falls all over Odysseus and wants him to go to bed with her (Homer doesn't seem to care that Odysseus is a married man) and has all her servants wash him and anoint him. You'd think he'd get tired of having other people wash him all the time and put oil all over him. (My parents don't want me to watch any sex or violence on television. If only they knew what the school is asking us to read!)

Anyway, Odysseus and his pig-men end up staying there twelve months!

Carl Ray happened to sneak by me in the living room while I was reading, and he asked me what part I was on. When I mentioned about Circe and the pigs, he said, "Oh yeah. Book Ten." This surprised the heck out of me. And when I said that I thought it was a little far-fetched about the men turning into pigs, he said, "Well, it's a metaphor." (Can you imagine Carl Ray even knowing what a metaphor *is*?) And I said, "How so?" and he said, "Women turn men into pigs all the time."

Then he went into the kitchen to make himself about four sandwiches.

And I sat there thinking about that. I hate to admit it, but it's really very interesting and I wondered why *I* didn't think of that. Maybe this whole trip that Odysseus is on is a big metaphor, you know, like the poem about the woods on the snowy evening. That road is supposed to be the road of life.

I asked Alex about it that night when we went to the movies (Beth Ann and Carl Ray went to play miniature golf), and even *he* seemed to have known all along about all the metaphors. He said, "Sure, his whole trip is a metaphor. It's like life, you know. All the time you're trying to find home *(you are?)* and all the time you have these adventures."

I never even knew that Alex paid attention in English. *I'm* supposed to be the one good in English. I felt pretty stupid. But I like the *Odyssey* better now.

I will tell only briefly about Saturday night because the thunder is scaring me to death.

We went to the movies and saw this really sappy romance, but I have to admit that I enjoy the kissing scenes a lot more now than I used to. I've been *studying* them. I think I might write my own manual. Usually the guy starts the kiss, but not always. If he starts it, the girl often acts shy at first, but then she gets into it, and throws her arms around his neck. When the girl starts it, the guy usually looks pleased, and then he throws *his* arms around *her*.

One odd thing I've noticed is that the kisses rarely occur when everything is all quiet and romantic. They happen at times you wouldn't ordinarily expect them, like after a fight—just when the woman has been telling the man that she hates him—or right in the middle of the street with people walking past and cars honking their horns. In the movie we saw tonight, a couple kissed right smack in the middle of the supermarket, after the woman picked up a frozen chicken! I've never noticed that in real life. Maybe it happens, though. Maybe I haven't been paying enough attention.

After the movie, Alex and I went to the park and he started telling me about why he likes basketball so much, but that he's always worried he won't make the team. Now, that surprised me about Alex. I thought he was Mr. Basketball Confidence. And right in the middle of talking about basketball, he reached over and put his arm around me. It's the *truth*! Now, how in the world do boys' brains work? How do they connect basketball and putting their arm around a girl? I would have liked a little warning. And what exactly is the girl supposed to *do* when the boy puts his arm around her? Just sit there? Move closer? Untangle her own arm and put it around him (squash!)?

I just sat there, pretending not to notice. Alex kept

talking about basketball. I was pretty sure the kiss was going to come next, but it didn't. Who cares??!! It's getting so that if Alex just breathes on me, I feel like I have on my magic sandals and am flying off to Mount Olympus. I think maybe Alex wasn't quite sure about this new move either, because after five minutes he moved that arm and then he scratched his head and then he leaned down and retied his shoe and then he stood up and stretched. I hope he didn't think that I *minded* about his arm. Was I supposed to say something? Like "It is nice of you to place your arm on my shoulder. You may keep it there if you like." Oh sighhhh. I'll change the subject.

Apparently Beth Ann and Carl Ray (I'm going to start calling him Lance Romance, as he is finally using the shower and splashing on tons of aftershave) had a "truly di-viiiiine and wonderful" time at miniature golf (how you could have a truly divine and wonderful time trying to push little balls through a clown's mouth is beyond me).

And Derek-the-jerk wasn't at the miniature golf range. Surprise, surprise.

Monday, July 23

Oh, brother. I don't believe it. That stupid Carl Ray.

At dinner tonight, Dad asked Carl Ray when he was going home and Carl Ray said he was leaving on Friday, and so Mom asked him when he would be back and he said the next Friday and then Dad asked him if he minded driving alone.

And Carl Ray said, "Don't rightly know."

And Dad said, "Mighty long drive."

And Mom said, "Isn't there anyone who could ride along with you?"

And then it went like this:

DAD: Good idea.
MOM: What about one of the kids?

Maggie looked at me and I looked at Dennis and he looked at Dougie and he looked at Tommy. Tommy said, "Me! Me! I going!"

MOM: No, Tommy, you're too little.
TOMMY: Me! Me!

Dad looked at Maggie.

MAGGIE: I'd like to, honest, but I just can't, what with watching Tommy and all, and besides, Kenny and I are going to the Easton Festival and also I promised Mrs. Furtz I would take Barry and Cathy and David and—

DAD: Okay, okay, I get the picture.

DENNIS: I'm going camping with Billy, remember?

MOM: Oh, right.

DOUGIE: And I get carsick. *(He really does.)*

Everyone, by this time, is looking at me. I am in a complete panic.

MOM: Oh, Mary Lou! Wouldn't you like to go?

ME: Sure. Sure, I'd really love to go and all, but boy, Maggie always needs help with Tommy, and Alex and I already made plans—

MOM: Plans? For what?

ME: Well, plans. To do stuff.

DAD: Like what?

ME: *(What was the matter with my stupid brain?)* Well, just plans. To go to the movies—

MOM: You just went to the movies.

ME: Another movie!

DAD: What else?

ME: You know, plans.

MOM: Well, really, Mary Lou, you might be the best

one to go, and besides, you've got the whole rest of the summer to see Alex.

ME: But—what about Alex? What if he forgets me? What if—

DAD: Absence makes the heart grow fonder.

And that was the absolute end of that. I couldn't believe it.

The only thing that makes me not pack my bag and run away from home is that Alex called tonight, and when I told him about having to go with Carl Ray, he said that that was amazing, because his parents had been bugging him to go with them to see his cousins in Michigan next Friday, Saturday, Sunday, Monday, and Tuesday, and that he'd been trying to find a way to convince them to let him stay home, but if I was going to be gone, he'd just go on with them.

That made me feel *a lot* better, but still—eight hours in a car with Carl Ray????

I do like to visit Aunt Radene, because they live on this great little farm with a cemetery in the front (they tell a lot of ghost stories) and a big hill in the back (with cows on it) and an enormous barn (with a loft full of hay) and the niftiest swimming hole in the world.

The bad part about visiting Aunt Radene is that not only is there no phone, but there also is no electricity and there is NO PLUMBING. That means outhouses and wells and stuff. Really.

But I don't know how I can be away from Alex for a whole week.

Beth Ann called to say that she had talked to Christy, who said that the GGP is still considering her for membership, but that she would have to come to the next pajama party, which is next Saturday. And Beth Ann said that since Carl Ray and I would both be gone (she sounded real jealous when she heard I was going, but I told her that he was just my stupid cousin and I didn't even want to go and it wasn't going to be any fun and I would remind him of her every five minutes), she might as well go to the GGP pajama party. Just for the heck of it, she said.

I'm glad I'll be gone.

Tuesday, July 24

My mother has forbidden me to use the following three words: "God," "stupid," and "stuff." She said I needed to expand my vocabulary. It's not easy eliminating those words all of a sudden. When she said that, I said, "Well, *God*!"

"Mary Lou!"

And then I said I had to go do the *stupid* dishes and she said, "Mary Lou!" and about two seconds later I said

I was going to have trouble not saying God and *stuff*, and she said, "Mary Lou!" So I asked her what in the heck I was supposed to do with these big holes in my vocabulary all of a sudden, and she said, "Use the thesaurus."

Right. So I spent about an hour combing the thesaurus, and here's what I came up with:

God: deity, Lord, Jehovah, Providence, Heaven, the Divinity, the Supreme Being, the Almighty, the Omnipotent, the Infinite Being, Alpha and Omega, the Absolute, King of Kings, etc. (There's lots more.)

(I'm having trouble picturing me saying, "Oh, deity!" or "Oh, Omnipotent!" or "Oh, Alpha and Omega!" but I'll give it a try.)

Stupid: foolheaded, asinine, buffoonish, apish, fatuous, witless, moronic, imbecile, batty, besotted, myopic, poppycockish, cockamamie, lumpish, oafish, boobish, beefbrained, chowderheaded, beetleheaded, cabbageheaded, etc.

(There are *lots* of words for stupid. I can't believe my mother wants me to use some of these, but I'll try. I practiced already: That witless ole Carl Ray! That beefbrained Christy! That cabbageheaded Beth Ann! Pretty good, eh?)

Stuff: material, constituents, sum and substance, nub, pith, quintessence, elixir, irreducible content.

(Well, *sure*. I can hear myself now. We all messed around and quintessence. He had all this elixir in his pocket. We went to the park and irreducible content. It doesn't make a bit of sense, if you ask me.)

Not much elixir happened today. Alex had to work all day, so I stayed home, watched Tommy, read some more *Odyssey*, and quintessence.

Mrs. Furtz came over again, all crying and nub, about some cabbageheaded letter she got. I don't know what she was going on about. I do feel sorry for her and all, I really do, but Omnipotent! She reallllllly gets to sobbing and pulling at her hair.

Alex and I are going out tomorrow night and Thursday night before our Separation. Oh, sob.

The only good thing about Carl Ray going out with Beth Ann is that after dinner he splashes on about a gallon of besotted aftershave and runs (well, drives) over to Beth Ann's (she lives a whole block away), and he doesn't get back until about ten or eleven o'clock. Dad is happy because he finally gets his TV-watching chair back, and everybody else is happy because they can watch their own programs again.

I have a confession to make. I snooped around in Carl Ray's room today. I don't know what got into me, but I was vacuuming upstairs and I was looking at all these new bottles of aftershave (he has *two* bottles of Canoe; he must have heard how much Beth Ann *loves* it) on his dresser, and his top drawer was open a bit and I sort of peered in and then I guess I was wondering if he had all his money in there and I wanted to see if he had any left, so I opened the drawer.

He sure had a lot of sum and substance in there. Alpha and Omega! About twenty packs of gum, a bunch of pennies and nickels, three can openers, two pocketknives, some horse chestnuts (???), three pairs of ratty old socks, pens, pencils, packs of matches, glue, a can of tuna fish (unopened), and a can of sardines (also unopened), a DIARY (!!!!), and something wrapped up in tissue paper.

I stared at the diary and the thing wrapped up in tissue paper for a few minutes. I didn't want anyone to catch me, but I sure wanted to open that diary and that little package. But I was starting to feel guilty. I decided to open only one thing. I figured that it would be worse to open the diary, so I opened up the tissue paper.

How peculiar.

Inside was a gold ring with a large black stone. There was also a card that said: "Carl Ray, I want you to have this. I'll explain later. C.F." I figured it must be from his father (Carl Joe Finney), but I never knew that Uncle Carl Joe could afford anything as fancy as that ring. If he could, why wouldn't he put a bathroom in his house?

I was going to look inside the ring to see if it had an inscription, but Dennis came upstairs then and he caught me sticking it back and asked what I was snooping at and I told him I was just cleaning, for Deity's sake.

The Dead

> *Book Eleven of the* Odyssey *is deadly boring. Ha. That's a pun, because this part is all about Odysseus's visit to the dead. It wasn't as exciting as I expected it to be. He meets some old friends who weren't as lucky as he (they're dead, after all) and also he meets a prophet who tells him what's going to happen to him in the future. He warns him about all the dangers ahead and tells him that he will kill all of his wife's suitors. I didn't think Homer should give away the ending like that. Also, this prophet tells Odysseus how he will die!!! He's going to die at sea, but a sort of peaceful death.*

Imagine. Would you want someone to tell you what was going to happen to you and how you were going to die? What if you were told you were going to die at sea? Wouldn't you stay about as far away from the sea as possible? But the way this prophet tells Odysseus, it's as if there isn't a darn thing he can do about it. It's all planned out. Would you want to know what was on your path of life and all? I wouldn't. No way. But I wouldn't mind visiting dead people. I'd check on how Mr. Furtz was doing.

Wednesday, July 25

I've just been with Alexxxxxx. Sigh. But I'll wait and tell about him at the end.

First, Beth Ann. She called today and jabbered on for hours about that wonnnnderful Carl Ray. That cabbageheaded ole Carl Ray sent her a dozen red roses!!! I asked her if she was absolutely sure they were from him, and she seemed a little offended. She said that there was a card with the flowers and it said, "To Cleo from Tony."

"Huh?" I said. "Cleo? Tony?"

She giggled. "Our nicknames. I'm Cleopatra, he's Antony."

Oh, Alpha and Omega! It took me about ten minutes to quit gagging. I could not imagine Carl Ray standing in some florist shop writing out this card that says, "To Cleo from Tony." I mean, what would the storekeeper *think*? King of Kings! Supreme Being! What *happens* to people?

But then I started wondering why Alex and I hadn't given each other nicknames, and then I started wondering if maybe he didn't like me as much as Carl Ray likes

Beth Ann, and then I started wondering why Alex hadn't sent *me* roses.

Anyway. Beth Ann still has not heard from "the jerk." If you ask me, she's too busy drooling over Carl Ray to care very much anymore. She sure forgot Derek-the-Divine quickly.

Oh, and Beth Ann, my devoted best friend, has definitely decided to go to the GGP pajama party on Saturday night when I am off in West Virginia suffering through a week of Carl Ray. Some friend.

So now Alex. Ah, Alex. Tonight I met him halfway between his house and my house, and then we walked back to his house. The Big Moment: I was going to meet his parents. All the way there, he told me about them. He said his dad would be very quiet and serious and that his mother would be a little weird. When I asked him what he meant by weird, he said she changes moods quickly and dresses strangely sometimes and never sits still, but that she was real nice anyway.

Mrs. Cheevey was standing in the driveway aiming a bow and arrow at the garage when we walked up. She was wearing a black cocktail dress, pearls, and a pair of tennis shoes. On her head was a baseball cap. She shot a bow and arrow at the garage door. It landed right between two of the windows. "Bull's-eye!" she shouted.

Then she heard us coming and turned around. "Oh

hi, hi, hi," she said, walking up to us. She was real pretty, with curly blond hair and a sweet round face.

She put her hand out to me. "Mary Lou, Mary Lou, Mary Lou!" she said. "That's right, isn't it?" She was smiling all over the place. She held out the bow and arrow. "Just practicing," she said. "Want to try?"

I said, "Maybe later," but I smiled a lot too.

"Well, come in, come in, come in," she said. So we followed her inside. Alex lives in this enormous house on Lindale Street. The living room is about as big as our whole downstairs, and it looks, at first, as if it should be a picture in a magazine. But then, if you look more closely, you notice some strange things. Each set of windows has a different color of curtains, for example: red, gold, purple, black, peach, blue. On one side of the room, the furniture is all antique-looking: a huge ornate couch in green velvety material, a gigantic wooden cupboard, four of those dainty little chairs that you would expect little princesses to be sitting on, and lots of those little round tables with curved legs. Then on the other side of the room, everything is modern: a long white couch, two leather-and-metal chairs that each look like an enormous S, and a long black coffee table with metal legs and a wavy top that looks like a great big noodle.

Then the walls. On the antique side is this orange-and-green-patterned wallpaper, and on the modern side the walls are shiny yellow. One side of the room (guess which side!) has six huge portraits of very stern-looking grandmothers and grandfathers (I guess).

The other side had all kinds of interesting things on it: one of those paintings that looks like someone just stood back and flicked paint off a spoon; a stuffed pig's head; a white plaster sculpture of an arm and hand coming right straight out of a piece of tin; a pair of red cloth lips, about two feet in diameter, with a stick of gum emerging from the center; and a long shelf (maybe six feet long) with hundreds and hundreds of little pebbles on it.

Mrs. Cheevey said, "Sit down, sit down, sit down," and she motioned us to the antique side of the room. We sat down. "Oh," she said, "I just love it, love it, love it, when Alex brings someone home!" Then she started calling for her husband, "Oh, Ralph, Ralph, Ralph."

Pretty soon Ralph came in. Wow! He is about seven feet tall, about as tall and skinny as anyone I have ever met. First I saw his feet coming down the stairs, and they were e-nor-mous. He wore gigantic leather sandals. Then I saw his legs coming down the stairs. He wore blue jeans, and his legs just kept coming and coming. I didn't think there was a body attached. Then I saw hands and arms hanging down: these long, swinging things in a red plaid shirt. Pretty soon a long neck and then, surprisingly, a rather small head. I was glad that it was a small head, because I was beginning to think a giant was coming down the steps. His face is pale and freckled and he has brown hair.

He stepped into the room. "Oh, Ralph, Ralph, Ralph," Mrs. Cheevey said, "this is Mary Lou!!" He nodded, but before he moved any farther, he motioned to the other side of the room with his hand. Alex and Mrs. Cheevey automatically got up, so I did too, and then we all went and sat on the other side of the room.

But as soon as we sat down, Mrs. Cheevey jumped back up and left the room. Mr. Cheevey said, "Son" (I liked that, the way he said "son," so formal and all), "do you and Mary Lou have plans for this evening?"

Alex said, "Yuh."

Then Mrs. Cheevey came rushing back in the room with a plate of oysters! Ugh. I'd never eaten oysters, and I didn't really feel like starting today, but it didn't look like I had any choice. She balanced the plate of oysters on two of the waves of the noodlelike table and went rushing out again. Then she came back in with some purple napkins (cloth) and handed us each one and sat down. Then she got back up and passed the plate of oysters around.

We had each swallowed one oyster when Mrs. Cheevey jumped up again and said, "Oh! Ralph, Ralph, Ralph! The time. It's so late, late, late." She was already up and halfway out of the room.

Alex said, “Well, I’m glad you got to meet—”

Mr. Cheevey stood up. “Mary Lou Finney,” he said, and put out his hand, and I quickly wiped off the oyster juice on my purple napkin and put my hand out and he gently crushed all my fingers in his enormous hand.

Already Mrs. Cheevey was back, carrying a green parka, which she put over her shoulders. She was still wearing the black cocktail dress, pearls, baseball hat, and tennis shoes. Mr. Cheevey was still wearing his jeans and plaid shirt and sandals. They left. Dressed like that, they left.

Alex said, “They’re really nice, honest, once you get to know them.”

“Wow,” I said.

Alex and I were *alone* in his house. I started examining all the things on the walls—the pig’s head and the shelf with all the pebbles on it and the big pair of red lips with the gum sticking out the center. Can you imagine practicing kissing on those huge lips?!! I think Alex was more nervous than I was, because he was shuffling all around. We did try sitting on the long, white couch, but we felt pretty silly sitting there on that huge couch in the middle of that enormous room, so finally Alex suggested we go to the Tast-ee Freeze. It was a relief, to tell you the truth. And then, just to show you that it must be true about the quiet, romantic places not being all that they are cracked up to be, wouldn’t you know it, when we got out on the street and were passing Artie's Automotive, that's when he put his arm on my shoulder again!

Here is something for my manual: When the guy puts his arm around the girl while walking along, the girl might find it more comfortable to also put her arm around him at this time. She can put it sort of across his back. It is a little difficult to walk this way, and you won't want to walk very far like this, but it's a neat thing to do. The girl will find it difficult to think of things to say during this time, but the boy will carry on about something or other (basketball, for example), and the girl can get by with saying, "Mmm" or "Ah" or "Oh?" This way she can concentrate primarily on not tripping.

When other people do these things, it looks so *easy*. Don't let that fool you.

Enough!

I leave for West Virginia with Carl Ray the day after tomorrow. Groannnn.

Temptations and Choices

Book Twelve of the Odyssey*: Wow! What an action-packed chapter. First, Odysseus and his men pass by the Sirens, who bewitch everyone who comes near them with their singing. Clever Odysseus blocks up his men's ears with wax. He wants to listen, though, so he* *has his men tie him up to the mast and orders them not to untie him, no matter how hard he might beg. If this is a metaphor, I think that the Sirens represent sexy women who tempt men (like Eve with Adam?). I don't think I am a Siren yet. I can hardly speak when I am with Alex, let alone sing!*

Then Odysseus's ship has to go between these two dangerous obstacles: One is Scylla, a horrible monster with twelve feet and six necks and six heads and three rows of teeth in each head, and she eats men from ships. The other obstacle is Charybdis, a whirlpool that sucks up whole ships. Odysseus can't get through without going close to one, but finally he decides to risk Scylla. Scylla snatches up about six of Odysseus's men and eats them up. I think that maybe Scylla and Charybdis represent two difficult choices, and that you have to take the choice that offers least harm. Maybe? Does that sound right?

Thursday, July 26

Ohhhhh, I have to leave tomorrow to go with beef-brained ole besotted Carl Ray.

And Beth Ann has been calling here all day, going on and on about how she can't *bear* to be apart from him and how I should remind him every day about her and on and on and on.

And Alex and I spent about four hours together at the park. We played tennis. It sure is a lot more fun playing tennis with Alex than with Beth Ann.

Alex pays attention and says things like "Great shot!" (about my shot, not his; Beth Ann would say it about her own) and "Whoa!" (if I zing one past him, which I can occasionally do), and he generally gives the impression that he is having a terrific time. We laugh if one of us "whiffs" the ball (that's what Alex calls it when you swing and miss), whereas with Beth Ann you have to pretend not to notice when she misses—and if *you* miss, she puts on this phony frown as if she feels so enormously sorry for you.

We were too sweaty to hold hands or anything afterward, but on the way home he said he would think about me a lot while he was gone and I said (yes, I actually got some mushy words out) that I would think about him a lot while I was gone. Oh sighhhh.

Is there such a thing as being *too* happy? It makes me feel a little guilty, especially when there are people like Mrs. Furtz who are feeling so awful. Speaking of Mrs. Furtz, the strangest thing happened tonight. Right after dinner, before Alex arrived, Mrs. Furtz came over. Mom and Dad were sitting at the kitchen table, I was washing the dishes, and Carl Ray was rummaging around in the refrigerator.

Mrs. Furtz looks terrible lately. I bet she hasn't combed her hair in a week, and she was wearing this old sweatshirt and a pair of baggy pants and crummy old shoes. You could tell she'd been crying. She sat down at the table with my parents and started sniffling.

Carl Ray stood there staring at Mrs. Furtz with this really sorrowful look on his face and then all of a sudden he left the room, and about two minutes later, he came downstairs with a tissue-wrapped package in his hand. He went right up to Mrs. Furtz and handed it to her. She looked at him strangely, and Carl Ray said, "For you," and then he went outside and got in his car and drove away!

Mom and Dad looked so surprised and Mrs. Furtz kept staring at the tissue and I was wondering what in the world had happened to Carl Ray's mind. Finally, Mrs. Furtz opened it. Sure enough, it was the ring from Carl Ray's drawer. I leaned over and said, "Where's the card?" and they all looked at me. Carl Ray had taken the card out. "Oh," I said, "I just thought there'd be a card."

Then Mrs. Furtz started sobbing and Mom started patting her on the back and Dad went to get a box of Kleenex, and that's when Alex came to the door.

Now what would make Carl Ray do something like that? Why would he give Mrs. Furtz his father's ring?

He's just full of surprises.

When I got home tonight, Dad was talking to Carl Ray and asking him if maybe he didn't want to reconsider and take the ring back, that it was a very nice gesture and that Mrs. Furtz was so overwhelmed she couldn't speak, but Carl Ray might regret his impulse, and if so, everybody would understand and Dad was sure that Mrs. Furtz would give the ring back.

When Dad was done with his little speech, Carl Ray just said, "Nope," and went to bed.

Oh, Alpha and Omega!

Friday, July 27

Oh, Deity! I'm here at Aunt Radene's in West Virginia and there is no light in the bedroom and I'm trying to write by the moonlight. I feel like Abraham Lincoln. I can't see hardly anything. I'll have to write tomorrow in the daytime. Oh, I miss home and Alex!!!

Saturday, July 28

Oh, King of Kings, what a day yesterday was and what a day today is turning out to be.

Right now, I'm sitting on Aunt Radene's and Uncle Carl Joe's front porch on this great red wooden swing that's screwed into the ceiling of the porch. Down in front of me is a hill and on it is the graveyard. Spoooooky.

I'll start with yesterday.

Carl Ray and I left home about noon. I was in charge of the map and he was in charge of the driving. Boy, Carl Ray drives like a maniac!! I was fearing for my life the whole time. He speeds along at about ninety miles an hour and swerves around cars to pass them and never uses his turn signals and he hates to stop. I had to beg him, after about four hours, to please stop so I could go to the bathroom.

We didn't talk hardly at all, thank goodness. I brought along the *Odyssey* and pretended to be engrossed in that. Every now and then he would ask me what part I was on, and when I told him he would say, "Oh, yeah, I liked that part," or "Oh, that's a good part." He really knows that book. I think he must have memorized it or something.

Anyway, we only got lost once, and we finally arrived at Aunt Radene's at nine o'clock. Aunt Radene and all of Carl Ray's brothers and sisters (Arvie Joe, John Roy, Lee Bob, Sue Ann, Sally Lynn, and Brenda Mae—everybody has two names, like me) were waiting on the porch and started jumping up and down and waving and acting like lunatics. The only one who wasn't there was Uncle Carl

Joe. At first I thought it was kind of nice, such a great reception and all, but then when we got out of the car, everyone jumped all over Carl Ray and started hugging him and messing his hair, and I realized they weren't at all excited to see *me.*

After about an hour of that, Aunt Radene finally noticed me standing there looking like an idiot, and she came over and hugged me and then everyone else did too, so it was about another half hour of people messing up *my* hair. They're sure a happy bunch.

Then we had to go in and eat dinner. Aunt Radene said, "Gosh, we're starving to death. We usually eat up at five, but we were waitin' on you all. Gosh, I'm as happy as a pumpkin in a patch to see you." That's just the way she talks, honest, I'm not making it up.

Uncle Carl Joe was already sitting at the kitchen table. He glanced up when Carl Ray came in, and everybody went all quiet and stared at the two of them. Then Carl Ray said, "Hey," and Uncle Carl Joe nodded, very soberly, and everybody started crowding around the table. It was pretty easy to tell that Carl Ray and his father were not on the best of terms.

About three tons of food was spread on the table: fried chicken, mashed potatoes, gravy, bread, green beans, squash, biscuits, tomatoes, corn, and peaches. Then for dessert: pecan pie and apple pie and molasses pie. For a family that seems poor as anything (like I said, no electricity and no plumbing and the house looks as if it hasn't been painted in about two hundred years), they sure have a lot of food on the table. I don't know how in the world Carl Ray was so skinny when he first came to our house.

Carl Ray had about ten helpings of food, which was a little embarrassing because he made it look like we never feed him.

Everyone kept asking Carl Ray what it was like in "The City" and I kept trying to say it isn't a city that we live in. Easton is just a little suburb; it's about ten miles from a big city. But they kept on and on about The City, asking him how many murders he'd seen and how many times he'd been held up by robbers and all that kind of sum and substance. Honestly.

They also kept asking Carl Ray about his car, and I thought he'd tell them about the money and the college education, but you could tell he was saving it for another time, because he looked real embarrassed whenever they mentioned it. They kept saying things like "You sure must make a lot of money in The City," and "Wow, Carl Ray, you're gonna be a millionaire," and on and on. It was as if he didn't *want* to tell them about the money.

Uncle Carl Joe didn't say a word.

Then, about ten thirty, when we had finished eating,

everybody got up and Aunt Radene said, "Best turn in; we can chaw on and on tomorrow." And in about ten minutes everybody was in bed, except for Sue Ann and Sally Lynn, who were doing the dishes. I did ask if I could help, but they said no, so I just went to bed. I was really tired and also feeling really homesick for everybody.

I wonder if Carl Ray felt this way when he came to stay with us. How did he stand it? Everybody's so *nice* to him here, and he's lapping it up like a little dog. And they're all looking at me as if *I'm* the strange one, and I can hardly get a word in, not that I would know what to say if I *did* get the chance. So I don't say too much—just like Carl Ray at our house. It makes you think, doesn't it?

It's a little hard to get used to how *primitive* this place is. I still haven't gone to the bathroom. I did walk out to the outhouse.

Oh, Supreme Being! I'd forgotten just how awful that outhouse is. It's so dark inside. The only light that can get in is a little sunlight from a hole cut high up one wall. But also through that hole come flies and wasps and creepy spiders. There are spiderwebs in all the corners. I don't even want to mention the *smell*. Arghhhh. I'll wait until I am absolutely desperate before I go in there. Maybe Carl Ray was as afraid of our bathroom as I am of his. Maybe he was used to all this back-to-nature sum and substance.

Later the same day

I'm back on the porch swing. I've been sitting here most of the day writing letters. Everybody else has been rushing around doing chores, and whenever I ask if I can help, they say, "Naw, you just set awhile."

I'm getting tired of "setting awhile."

Still later the same day

I think Aunt Radene has the flu.

She did make dinner tonight though. We had fried chicken (again, because it's Carl Ray's favorite), gravy, boiled potatoes, corn on the cob, tomatoes, sweet potatoes, and fried peppers. Then for dessert we had chocolate pudding with whipped cream and also cherry Jell-O with bits of peaches inside.

We almost didn't get the pudding because Aunt Radene dropped it. Arvie Joe was asking Carl Ray if he was *sure* he hadn't seen any murders yet in The City, and Carl Ray said, "The only dead body I've seen was—" but he didn't finish because that's when the pudding slipped out of Aunt Radene's hands. She doesn't like to hear about dead people—I can tell.

Then, while Aunt Radene was scooping up the pudding, Arvie Joe asked Carl Ray about his job in the hardware store, so Carl Ray told them about stocking and orders and all that boring quintessence. Arvie Joe said, "They sure must pay you a lot, if you can afford that car."

Carl Ray looked right at me, and I knew it was a warning, so I didn't say anything—not until Arvie Joe kept going *on* about how much money Carl Ray must be earning. Just to *participate* a little in the conversation, I said, "Well, Carl Ray's lucky. People keep *giving* him things—"

Carl Ray gave me a dirty look.

"Like what?" Sally Lynn said.

I was in trouble now. I fished around and fished around. "Well, like a job . . ." (Carl Ray relaxed a little) ". . . and a ring . . ." (Carl Ray gave me the dirty look again).

"A ring?" said Aunt Radene.

I was about to explain that it was the ring from Uncle Carl Joe, but then Uncle Carl Joe said, "A ring? What the blazes for?" Everybody looked at Uncle Carl Joe. I think those were the first words he said to Carl Ray since we arrived. I couldn't tell if Uncle Carl Joe was pretending he hadn't given the ring to Carl Ray or if he thought I meant that Carl Ray had been given *another* ring.

Carl Ray was staring at me. Then I realized that Carl Ray knew that the only way I could have known someone had given that ring to him in the first place was if I had been snooping in his drawers and read that card. I tried to move on. I said, "Oh well, he gave it away anyway."

"You gave it away?" said Aunt Radene to Carl Ray.

"You gave it *away*?" said Lee Bob and Sue Ann.

"What did you go and give the ring away for?" asked Uncle Carl Joe.

But it was about this time that Aunt Radene fainted dead away on the floor (fortunately she missed the pudding mess), and Uncle Carl Joe and Sue Ann and Lee Bob all jumped up and started patting her face and everybody else was crowding around and then they carried her into her bedroom.

Carl Ray stayed in the room with her and the rest of us went back out and ate dessert. Sally Lynn said we could eat the pudding because the floor was "clean enough to eat up off of" and it "wouldn't hurt us none." It was good, even though I did find a dog hair in mine, but I didn't tell anyone.

So then Sue Ann, Sally Lynn, and Brenda Mae did the dishes (I asked if I could help, but they said no) and now everybody's getting ready for bed and I'm sitting here in the kitchen writing by the kerosene lamp. Aunt Radene is still in bed, but I can hear her voice. She's talking to Carl Ray, so she must feel a little better.

I sure would like to know why Uncle Carl Joe seems

so mad at Carl Ray and why they don't talk to each other. And I sure would like to know when Carl Ray's going to tell everybody about the money and the college education. Maybe he wants them all to believe that he is making a ton of money working in a hardware store.

I'm going to the outhouse. I can't put it off any longer. If I don't come back, tell Alex I lovvvve him. And my parents too. And Maggie, Dennis, Dougie, and Tommy.

Sunday, July 29

(I survived the outhouse.)

After breakfast, I went with Lee Bob, Sue Ann, and Sally Lynn to the swimming hole. It is the greatest place in the world. You have to climb a big hill out back and then go through some woods and then down a steep hill by way of a narrow path, and at the bottom of this hill is a creek and you follow the creek along for a while and then you come to the swimming hole. It's not very big, maybe fifteen feet across, but it's pretty deep in the middle. There are trees hanging over it, so when you float on your back, you can look up and see tons of leaves. All around the edges are old fallen logs. One of these sticks out into the water and Lee Bob dives off it. No one else is brave enough to.

Well, we were having a great time. I thought I was in a magical place. But all of a sudden, Lee Bob yells "Snapper!" and everybody starts flailing around trying to get to shore. I didn't know *what* was going on. They were all yelling at me to get out and hurry up and, boy oh boy, I scrambled out so fast.

They were all pointing over to one side. "What is it?" I kept saying.

"Snapper! Snapper!"

"What's a snapper?"

They all looked at me like I was an imbecile.

"Snapping turtle, dummy," Lee Bob said.

"You mean there's a snapping turtle in *there*?" I said.

"Couple of 'em. You gotta watch it or they'll get your toes."

After a while, everybody went back in the water. Everybody but me. I'd had enough swimming for one day.

I was suddenly reminded of Mr. Furtz. Swimming in that hole all happy and everything and then hearing "Snapper!" reminded me of how we were going along all cheery as clams when the phone rang that day and we found out Mr. Furtz was dead. *Snapper!* It makes you a little afraid to get back in the water. Is that a metaphor?

I'm the same age as Sally Lynn, but the funny thing is that even though I'm from The City, she and Sue Ann seem a lot older than I am. They're always talking about boys, and you can tell from the way they talk that they've been going out with boys for a *long* time. Sue Ann said that three of her best friends, who are the same age as she is, are engaged to be married!!!! Imagine!!! And Sue Ann's best friend, who is sixteen years old, is pregnant! And no one seems to mind! Some things seem a little advanced here in West Virginia. What's the *hurry*??? My mother would have a fit.

Sue Ann and Sally Lynn kept asking me about Alex, but I kept trying to change the subject, because I knew they would want to know what-all we did (in the way of messing around) and I was pretty sure they'd think that what Alex and I did was pretty babyish. I mean, if they knew that we hadn't even *kissed*, they would laugh themselves silly. Maybe Alex will kiss me when I get back. I ought to practice.

The Disguise

I've been "settin'" on the porch reading the Odyssey. *Odysseus finally reaches Ithaca (his home), and instead of going right to his house (as I would have) he goes to an old shepherd's hut, disguised as a beggar.*

Telemachus (his son) comes along, and at first

Odysseus goes on pretending he is a beggar, but then finally he lets his son know who he is. That's a nice part, because they both start crying and all. I liked Odysseus better then, because I was beginning to wonder if he had any feelings. It was beginning to seem like all he did was sack cities and poke out the eyes of monsters and go on and on about how clever he was.

Later

Aunt Radene said she was feeling "a mite better," but she didn't look well at all. Her eyes were all puffy and even her freckles were pale.

Do you know what she asked me? (Of course you don't.) She said that Carl Ray told her all about the money he received at Mr. Biggers's office and about the college education. "Any idea who that was from?" she asked.

"Nope," I said.

"Well," she said, "I'm gonna ask you something strange, and if'n you'd rather not do what I'm gonna ask you, you just tell me straight on out and I'll abide by that. But if'n you'll do what I ask, I'd be beholden, Mary Lou Finney."

I love the way she talks. And I think I understood what she said.

So she went on, “Now, Carl Ray has told me about gettin’ this money and a education from some stranger, like I said, and I know you know about that already.”

I was nodding.

“So what I want to ask you is this: I want to ask you not to tell Uncle Carl Joe or any of the kids about Carl Ray gettin’ this money and all. Would you do that for me?”

I said, “Sure, Aunt Radene. I won’t tell if you don’t want me to.”

She patted my hand.

“But,” I said, “could you tell me *why* you don’t want me to tell?”

She chewed on her lip awhile and then said, “Well, now, that’s a fair question. It sure is.” She chewed on her lip some more. I have a feeling she didn’t want to tell me.

Finally, she said, “There’s just some things that ain’t nobody’s business, at least not yet, and the way I figure it is this: Carl Ray’s been lucky and he’s had some good fortune, but if the rest of ’em hear about some stranger givin’ him money and all, then they’re gonna want to troop on up to The City too. And Mary Lou, I don’t want ’em to go. Not yet. I don’t want ’em to go, ’cause I might not get ’em back.”

Well, it sounded reasonable to me, so I agreed.

But I do wonder why she doesn’t even want to tell

Uncle Carl Joe. You'd think that Carl Ray's own father ought to at least know about it. Maybe he would have an idea who gave Carl Ray the money. Maybe it's some old army buddy of his or something. Maybe it's some long-lost maiden aunt of Uncle Carl Joe's who is about a hundred years old.

So I'm going to keep the secret, but there's something funny about all this, don't you think?

Boy, am I homesick!! I sure wish I could call home.

And later

Arghhh. Arvie Joe has been telling ghost stories out on the porch. He claims that every single one of them is true, and all the ghosts come from the graveyard in the front yard.

The worst one was about this young boy who got his head chopped off in some freak accident at a meat factory and how his body is always roaming around the yard looking for his head, and how his head is always somewhere around moaning and calling for his body. Oh, the noises Arvie Joe can make! He imitates the head calling for the body: "Ohhhhhh, bod-eeeee, where are youuuu?" He makes the head sound real sorrowful and gruesome, just the way a head might sound, I guess, if it was looking for its body. Anyway, right near the end of this story,

Arvie Joe jumps up all of a sudden and gets this god-awful look on his face, and his mouth hangs open and he starts backing away from us and pointing out into the yard, and we all look out there and Arvie Joe says, "There it is. The *head*! There it is!" And we all look, but we can't see anything, it's so pitch black out there, and then Arvie Joe starts screaming and saying, "It's *coming*, watch out, it's *coming*!" and we all run into the house, screaming and shaking.

Uncle Carl Joe was sitting there in his chair, chewing his tobacco, when we all came running in. "Arvie Joe!" he said. "Quit scarin' 'em, or I'll tan you one." But everybody was peering out the window and telling Uncle Carl Joe that the head was coming, and all of a sudden Uncle Carl Joe made these awful noises, just like Carl Ray did that day he chased me and Dennis and Dougie and Tommy at Windy Rock, and then he started chasing us around, and then Arvie Joe and Carl Ray joined in.

Boy, I mean to tell you I was scared about to death, with these three guys growling and chasing us, and the whole time I kept looking around for the head of that boy because I thought it might be chasing us too.

Boy, this is one strange family.

But you know what? It was the first time I've seen Uncle Carl Joe and Carl Ray doing something together and having fun. Afterward I saw the two of them walk down toward the graveyard together. I think they were actually *talking.*

And I'll tell you one thing: I am *not* going to the outhouse at night anymore, flashlight or no flashlight. I'll just have to wait until everyone's asleep and use the pot that's under the bed. Oh, Alpha and Omega, when will I be able to go home???

Monday, July 30

Oh yawn, yawn, yawn. I am so tired I could sleep standing up. I didn't get any sleep last night.

First I had to wait until Sue Ann, Sally Lynn, and Brenda Mae were asleep (we're all in the same room) so I could use the pot under the bed. Then I had one heck of a time trying to use that dumb thing, and just when I finished and I stood up, I tripped and knocked it over, and what a mess. So I had to sneak downstairs to find some rags to mop it up with.

And when I got downstairs, I heard Aunt Radene and Uncle Carl Joe arguing in their bedroom. Actually, I could only hear Uncle Carl Joe. He was saying something about "my blasted son." I hope he didn't mean Carl Ray, and I hope they're not mad at each other again. I was afraid they'd hear me and think I was snooping, so I went back upstairs, and the only thing I could think of to mop up the pee with was my socks, so I blotted it all up and stuck the socks in the pot and pushed it back under the bed.

Then I couldn't go to sleep because I kept thinking that the boy's head was going to come in the open window (I sleep right next to the window), so I shut the window, but then I kept thinking that the head could still *look* in the window, and if it was a ghosthead maybe it could come *through* the window. So I put my head under the sheets.

Then I was pretty sure I could hear the head out there moaning. I thought I heard it say, "Oh, bod-eee, where are youuuu?"

I must have dozed off finally, because I had this awful nightmare. In it Mr. Furtz's dead body was running all around the yard looking for his head, or at least that's what I thought it was looking for, because it didn't have a head on it. I was sitting in a tree (why was I sitting in a tree?) and then I happened to look next to me, and there, on the branch, was a head. The head fell out of the tree and landed on the body with a sickening glump, and I woke up. Thank the Deity!!! I was shaking to death. And then I noticed that the window was open.

I really want to go *home.*

Oh, and at breakfast this morning, cabbageheaded ole Sue Ann says, "Oh, Mary Lou, are you missing a pair of socks?"

"No."

"Well, I found a pair of yours . . ."

"I'm not missing any socks."

". . . in the pee pot."

Everybody started snorting in their oatmeal.

"*After* I peed in it," she said.

Everybody was rolling off their chairs.

Arvie Joe said, "Normally, we don't put our socks in the pee pot. . . ."

And everybody's gagging and snorting and rolling around.

Aunt Radene finally made them all shut up.

Boy, I can't wait to go home.

Tuesday, July 31

Lordie. The last day of July. Summer's almost over.

About the most exciting thing that has happened so far today is that Arvie Joe took me along on his paper route this morning.

First, we got in this old truck that looks as if it was the first truck ever made, and we drove down to the general store to pick up the papers. Arvie Joe isn't really old enough to drive, but he does anyway. He's pretty good at it, too. Then we sat outside the general store folding the papers. You have to fold them in thirds and tuck one end inside the other so that when you throw them they don't go flying all over the place.

It's not like doing a paper route in Easton, where you just walk along and place a paper in front of everybody's door. We're so way out in the country here that you have to drive and drive—sometimes it's at least three miles between houses. The houses are set pretty far back from the road, so Arvie Joe slows way down and then whips the paper out the window and up to the front porch. Boy, does he have good aim.

He did the first few houses himself, to show me how. If the house is on the left side of the road, it's easy—he just whips the paper straight out his window. But if it's on the right side of the road, he has to whip the newspaper up over the roof of the truck.

After he showed me how, he let me do the houses on the right side. I messed up the first few. I threw one in a birdbath, one about halfway up the lawn, and another one hit a chicken in the front yard. But Arvie Joe was real nice about it.

He said, "Don't they teach you how to throw, up there in The City?"

I said that it wasn't high on the list of things to teach kids, no.

"Well, it oughtta be," he said. Then he asked me

what was high on the list of things to teach kids. I had to think awhile. "I guess algebra and English and stuff." (I didn't think "sum and substance" would go over real well with Arvie Joe.)

"Besides school crud," he said.

"Well, besides school crud, let's see . . . swimming, maybe. Baseball, I guess. Tennis."

"*Tennis?* God almighty."

"Anything wrong with tennis?"

"Sissy game."

"Ah."

"What else?"

"That's about it."

"God almighty. What about your parents? Don't they teach you stuff, like throwin' and fixin' cars and stuff?"

I had a hard time with that one. "Manners, I guess. My parents are big on manners."

"*Manners?* God almighty, girl. *Manners?* Manners sure ain't gonna help you when you gotta fix a car!"

He was dying laughing.

Anyway, that was the big excitement of the day, Arvie Joe's paper route.

I've hardly seen Carl Ray at all since we got here. He's always off in his car, visiting his friends. He has a ton of friends here. That surprised me, I guess. And I keep forgetting to remind him about Beth Ann. I'd better do that. Maybe he'll want to leave if I start reminding him about his Cleopatra back in Easton.

It's funny, but the first day we were here, Carl Ray seemed so happy and excited to be back. But the last couple days, he seems so quiet when he's here (which, as I said, isn't all that much). He talks to Aunt Radene a lot, and ever since he and Uncle Carl Joe had their walk in the graveyard, they seem nicer to each other. But they still don't actually talk to each other, in front of me, anyway.

Well, I'm going to stop for now. John Roy and Sally Lynn just asked me if I wanted to climb up Booger Hill (the hill right behind the barn) with them. I have no idea why it's called Booger Hill.

Later

I'm sooooo homesick. I really want to go home.

So I went, this afternoon, with John Roy and Sally Lynn to climb Booger Hill. They had packed some bologna sandwiches and Kool-Aid in a backpack, so we could have a picnic at the top.

John Roy was leading. He claimed we were following a path, but I couldn't really *see* a path. On the way through the woods, they were telling me about a prisoner who escaped from a nearby prison two days ago. They were saying that he was armed and very dangerous. He's killed all kinds of people, John Roy said.

"You don't think he'd be around here, do you?" I asked.

"Naw," John Roy said. "Why would he pick *this* hill? There's millions of other hills he could hide out on."

Sally Lynn said, "But he *could* have picked this hill, John Roy. He *could* have. Maybe he's scared. Maybe he didn't know which way to go. Maybe he's starving to death."

"Naw," John Roy said. "If he's such a good killer, he could kill all kinds of animals. He won't be starvin'."

"But he *could* be," Sally Lynn said.

We climbed and climbed. I was getting a little tired, and my feet were killing me. I just had these cockamamie sandals on, but they were wearing work boots.

After we'd been walking for about an hour, John Roy said, "We're almost to the cabin. We could eat there."

"Cabin?"

"It's sort of run-down and fallin' to bits," Sally Lynn said.

Pretty soon John Roy says, "There it is," and he points to this pile of logs covered by some tarpaper. If you looked real hard, you could imagine that one time maybe it did look like a cabin.

We had just come up to the door (well, actually,

there was no door, only a door*way*) and John Roy said, "Whoa!" and Sally Lynn gasped and backed right into me, and I said, "What is it? What's the matter?"

John Roy whispered, "Somebody's been here. Look." He pointed to some charred logs on the ground in front of the doorway. "That's recent," he whispered.

Then Sally Lynn said, "Lord Almighty, gum wrappers!" Then, before I could really see the gum wrappers, John Roy said, "Let's get out of here," and Sally Lynn yelped, and they took off running.

John Roy dropped the backpack with the lunch inside.

"Waitttttt!" I shouted, but they didn't even turn around; they just kept on running, so I took off after them.

John Roy shouted back, "Quit shouting! It's the convict. He's here."

Once, in the fifth grade, I won first place in the hundred-yard dash at the school sports day. I ran like the wind that day. But compared to today, I bet that fifth-grade dash was a turtle crawl. I ran like crazy. I was sure that convict was going to reach out from behind any tree and grab me.

The worst part was that I couldn't see either John Roy or Sally Lynn anymore. I could hear people running, but I couldn't see them and I sure couldn't see any path and I was just running and running. All I knew was that I was aiming downhill, but I had no idea where I was going other than down. Then I lost my sandal, but I kept on running. I was afraid that I was running right straight toward the convict or he was right behind me.

I ran and ran. It seemed like forever before I came to a creek at the bottom of the hill, but it wasn't the place where we had started climbing. No sign of John Roy or Sally Lynn. I was sure the convict had already caught them. I figured I was going to have to find some help quick. I ran along the stream, thinking it had to lead *somewhere*, and finally I came to the swimming hole, so I knew where I was. I ran all the way up that hill, and when I saw the house, I started shouting for help and screaming my stupid lungs out.

Aunt Radene came out of the house and I was flailing my arms around, telling her about the convict and how he must have got John Roy and Sally Lynn and we had to get the police right away. I was so out of breath, I thought I was going to pass out.

The whole time I was trying to explain, Aunt Radene stood there looking at me as if I had lost all my marbles. Finally, she said, "Shh, come on inside."

I didn't want to go inside. I wanted her to hurry up and get some help and I wanted her to run, not poke along like she was doing. Then, all of a sudden, I see John

Roy and Sally Lynn come strolling out of the house, each one drinking a glass of lemonade.

"Where you *been*, Mary Lou?" John Roy asked.

"Yeah, where you *been*?" said Sally Lynn.

I stared at them. "Where have *I* been? Where have I been? Where in Alpha and Omega's name have *you* two been?" I thought I was going to faint dead away right there.

"Alpha and Omega?" said John Roy.

"What are you talkin' about?" said Sally Lynn.

"The *convict*!" I said. "Where'd you go? I lost you—"

"Looks like you lost your *shoe*," said John Roy.

"Yeah, where's your shoe at?" said Sally Lynn.

Aunt Radene was standing there, looking from them to me and back again. "John Roy," she said. "Sally Lynn—"

But then I went crazy. I ran inside and upstairs and fell on the bed and I bet I sobbed for fifteen minutes. After a while I heard Aunt Radene come up and say, "Mary Lou," but I pretended like I was asleep. Then I did fall asleep, and I slept right up until dinnertime, but I decided not to go downstairs. I decided I wouldn't eat until Carl Ray promised to take me home.

Carl Ray is the one who finally came upstairs to tell me dinner was ready. I pretended to be asleep, but he sat down in the chair by the bed and picked up my *Odyssey* and started reading. Finally, I decided to open my eyes or they were going to start twitching.

I said, "What part are you on?"

"Where Telemachus realizes who the beggar is."

"Oh yeah. And Telemachus and Odysseus cry. Carl Ray? Can we go home?"

"I *am* home."

"I mean to *my* home. Can we go back? Pleeeassse?"

I thought I was going to start crying again.

He nodded.

"Does that mean . . . ?"

"We're going on Friday—"

"But couldn't we go *before* Friday? Please? You could go out with Beth Ann then. Don't you think you should get back? What if Beth Ann finds somebody else?"

"Somebody else?"

"Yeah. Like what if her old boyfriend comes back?"

"Old boyfriend?"

"Well, gosh, Carl Ray, you're not her *first* boyfriend." I guess I shouldn't have said that. He looked sad.

"Can't go before Thursday."

"Okay then, Thursday. Could we leave Thursday?"

"Yup."

Oh, I wanted to jump up and kiss that cabbage-headed Carl Ray! I felt better just knowing we could leave one day sooner. So I went downstairs with Carl Ray for dinner. Carl Ray is okay.

I thought everybody would fall all over themselves teasing me about Booger Hill and the convict, but Aunt Radene must have threatened them, because no one said a word to me all through dinner. John Roy and Sally Lynn didn't say anything to anyone at all. They just stared down at their plates.

We're going home Thursday!!! Day after tomorrow!!!

Wednesday, August 1

What a horrible morning. I can't wait to get out of here. I don't care if I never come here again.

First of all, I woke up with a headache and an earache. The headache was from not getting much sleep again. I had horrible dreams about being on a ship and I was trying to get home and there was this awful storm that made the ship toss and roll around and we couldn't see where we were going. Carl Ray was there—I think he was the captain.

Anyway, I just knew I was going to die before I got home. I kept praying to Athene to please let me get home, and if she got me home, I would be a much better person. I woke up before we ever got anywhere, so I don't know what would have happened. I didn't want to go to sleep again, because I was afraid I would be back on the ship. So I lay there thinking about Alex and Mom and Dad and Maggie, Dennis, Dougie, and Tommy. I tried to picture their faces and hear their voices.

The earache is from swimming in the swimming hole, I think. It hurts so bad, I can hardly open my mouth. I tried to get Aunt Radene to take me to the doctor, but she said an earache was no reason to go to the doctor. I told her I might be dying. She said she had a remedy. Do you know what she poured in my ear? Olive oil! Honestly. I'm not a salad.

And I still have the earache.

But worse yet was what I heard Sue Ann and Sally Lynn saying about me.

I came back in from the outhouse, and I was about to go upstairs when I heard Aunt Radene's voice in the living room. I thought I would go in and tell her that my earache wasn't any better, but I stopped when I heard Sue Ann say, "And she's such a *baby*."

Then it went like this:

AUNT RADENE: Well, now, that's still no reason to—

SALLY LYNN: Lordie, Momma, she doesn't do a stitch of work.

SUE ANN: Have you seen her wash a single dish?

SALLY LYNN: And she doesn't make up her bed.

SUE ANN: *I* have to make up her stupid bed.
SALLY LYNN: All she does is lie around and read.
SUE ANN: Or write letters.
SALLY LYNN: I'm just sick of her.
SUE ANN: Me too.
SALLY LYNN: She thinks she's a queen.
SUE ANN: She sure does.
SALLY LYNN: Miss City Girl, Queen of Easton.

Well, I didn't hear any more, because I ran outside and up to the barn and climbed up in the hayloft and sat there. Boy, was I *mad*. I was *really* mad.

First of all, the dishes: I have offered at least five times to help with the dishes, and they keep saying, "No, you go set awhile."

Secondly, the bed: They don't give me a *chance* to make it up. I get out of bed, get dressed, go downstairs, eat breakfast, and I come back up and it's already made. I figured they *liked* to make it.

Thirdly: I am *not* a baby!!! I've only been crying because I am homesick and because they've been teasing me and scaring me to death.

Fourthly: Haven't done a stitch of work!! They never *asked* me to do *any*thing. I would've helped if they had *asked*.

Fifthly: All I do is write letters and read books! Well,

what else is there to do around this place????

Sixthly: I do *not* act like the Queen of Easton!!!!!

I stayed up in the hayloft a long time. After I got through being mad, I started to think about Carl Ray.

I hereby apologize for complaining about making Carl Ray's bed, for teasing him, and for calling him stupid, cabbageheaded, witless, beefbrained, boobish, besotted, cockamamie, and anything else I might have called him.

But I'm never going to speak to Sue Ann or Sally Lynn again.

Later

I didn't speak to Sue Ann or Sally Lynn all afternoon.

Instead, while Aunt Radene was off doing the grocery shopping, and Sue Ann and Sally Lynn were God knows where, I swept the front porch (without anybody asking); I mopped the kitchen floor (without anybody asking); I dusted the entire downstairs (without anybody asking); I cleaned the living room (without anybody asking); I picked some flowers from the hill and put them around the house (without anybody asking); I swept and dusted the bedroom that I share with Sue Ann, Sally Lynn, and Brenda Mae (without anybody asking); and I was just starting on the windows (without anybody asking) when

Aunt Radene drove up.

"Why, Mary Lou, what are you doin'?" she asked.

"Nothing. Washing windows."

She said, "You don't have to do that. You just set . . ."

"I don't *want* to set!" I said.

"But you're our *guest*," she said.

"Tough," I said.

When I finished the windows, I walked through the graveyard. It's a strange thing, walking through a graveyard in the daytime. It's not spooky, like it is at night. And it gives you this strange feeling: sort of a calm feeling in one way, and a very sad feeling in another way. When you're in a graveyard, all the other stupid things like the convict and the things Sally Lynn and Sue Ann said, all those things seem ridiculous to worry about. And you wonder why you worry about them and why you let them get you so mad.

The graveyard is a pretty place, with flowers here and there, with all that grass, with those stones and the poems and sayings written on them, all about loving memory and loving parents and loving sisters and loving brothers and time and heaven and sleep.

And I was so calm after walking around the graveyard that I lay down in the grass and fell asleep.

I dreamed a strange dream. It was about Carl Ray and some man with a sheet over his head, and Carl Ray was walking up to him in slow motion, and then he was lifting the sheet, and then the sheet was off and Carl Ray was hugging the man. And someone was calling me, "Mary LOUUU, Mary Louuuu, where are youuuu?" and then I woke up.

Aunt Radene was standing on the porch calling me.

So I went up to the house, and she said, "It's dinner-time. Come on in."

Boy, what a huge dinner. Fried chicken (again), mashed potatoes, corn on the cob, tomatoes, green beans, coleslaw, potato salad, and beets. Everybody was talking about how it was Carl Ray's last night home (they didn't mention *me*) and oh, they wished he would stay longer, and couldn't he at least stay until Saturday, and I started to feel sick because I thought he might give in and say yes.

But then. It was time for dessert. Sally Lynn and John Roy went into the living room and came out with this huge chocolate cake and on it, in huge white letters, was "MARY LOU: WE'LL MISS YOU."

And then everybody started talking to me all at once, and Sally Lynn said she was sorry about Booger Hill and John Roy said he was sorry about the convict and Sue Ann said she was sorry if I overheard them today (how did she know?) and that they didn't mean it, and on and on. I thought I was going to cry, but I didn't want to seem like a *baby*, so I chewed on my lip a lot.

That was a nice thing for them to do, don't you think?

But still, I'm not sorry to leave and WE GO HOME TOMORROW!!!!!!!

HOORAY!!!!

Thursday, August 2

I AM HOME!!!!!!!!!!!!!!!

We made it! The ship didn't crash in the storm. Captain Carl Ray got us through. I am in my OWN room writing at my own NEW DESK. But, but, but. There's more to tell first.

Where oh where to begin? Calm down, Mary Lou.

The trip. You can imagine, I guess, that I wasn't real sorry to leave Aunt Radene's, even if she did cry when she hugged me good-bye and even if Sally Lynn did give me a present (a book wrapped up in paper: it's all about sex) and even if Aunt Radene did hold on to Carl Ray as if she wasn't ever going to see him again.

One really surprising thing is that Carl Ray and I talked (yes, *talked*) on the way back, and I found out the most amazing things about Carl Ray.

First, I asked him if he had ever been homesick at our

house, and he said yes. So I asked him why he hadn't said anything about being homesick, and he said, "Wouldn't have done any good, would it?" I had to think about that. When I asked him if he would *still* be homesick now, he said he didn't rightly know. "But why are you coming back, then?" He said he had some "unfinished business," and he wouldn't explain, but I figure he means Beth Ann.

It took about a hundred miles of the trip to get that much out of Carl Ray. Then I asked him if Uncle Carl Joe was always mad at him.

"Mad?" he said. "What do you mean, 'mad'?"

"Well, he didn't exactly seem thrilled to see you home."

Carl Ray gave me one of his long, mournful looks. "He just doesn't show it," he said. "We had a fight."

"A fight?" This was interesting.

"Before. When I was still living there. That's why I left in such a hurry. That's why I came to Easton."

"What? You didn't come to find work? Aunt Radene said you were coming to look for work."

"I did look for work, didn't I?" he said.

"But what was the fight *about*?" Carl Ray gets away from the important issues very quickly.

"Well . . ." He looked as if he was trying to decide whether or not he should continue. "If I tell you something, do you promise not to . . ."

Oh boy, here we go again, I thought. Maggie and Beth Ann are always making me promise not to tell. And Aunt Radene asked me to keep the secret about Carl Ray. Now someone else making me promise not to tell. I can't keep all these promises straight.

"I *promise.* Now just tell me."

"You really can't repeat—"

"I *promised*, didn't I? God, Carl Ray."

"Naw," he said. "I can't. Mom would kill me."

"Carl Ray! That's so mean. First you make me promise. Then I promise. Now you're not going to tell me. God." (I was saying "God" again.)

But he wouldn't tell me. So I was mad for a while. Then I decided to read the *Odyssey*, but all of a sudden I remembered the dream in the graveyard and all of a sudden I realized that Carl Ray was Telemachus!!! I said, "I've been having the strangest dreams, and you're in almost every one."

"Me?" He looked pleased.

Then I told him each dream. I told him about the headless body dream and the ship in the storm dream and then the graveyard dream where he rips the sheet off of the man and starts hugging him. "I think I've been reading the *Odyssey* too much."

But Carl Ray had the strangest look on his face. His mouth was half open and his hands were wrapping tighter and tighter around the steering wheel.

"What's the matter, Carl Ray?"

"That's amazing," he said.

"What is?"

He just sat there. I thought I was going to have to slap him or something. Then he said, "Okay. I'm gonna tell you. But you have to promise."

"I already promised. I am not promising again. If you don't believe me—"

"Okay. Okay. Here it is, then."

Why can't people just say things straight out? It drives me one hundred percent cra-zeeeee when they mumble around like this.

Ooops. Mom wants me to stop writing and talk with her.

Later

I'm too tired to finish this. Tomorrow. I have a lot to tell.

Friday, August 3

Oh, mercy. Why is everything getting so *complicated*? How am I ever going to catch up? How am I going to explain it?

And where, oh where, is Alexxxxx?????

Oh, God. I mean Alpha and Omega. Control yourself, Mary Lou. Back to the car trip home yesterday with Carl Ray.

Right.

Here is what Carl Ray told me when he finally decided that he could trust me. He said, "Have you ever thought your parents weren't your parents?"

"Sure," I said. "I always think I'm probably adopted. Only my parents don't want to tell me. See, they want to pretend—"

"Well, I never thought that."

"That I was adopted?"

"No. That *I* was adopted."

"Carl Ray, *are* you? Are you *adopted*? Is that what you're trying to tell me? If that—"

"No."

"No *what*? Carl Ray, just spit it out. Just spit it right out!!!" I was getting that exploding feeling again.

"I'm *trying* to. You know that fight I mentioned? The one with my father? Well. This is what it was about."

He talks so *slowly*! He pauses after every couple of words.

"One day my mother told me that my father was not my father, and then I went sort of crazy and left home—I was staying with some friends—and I didn't want to talk to my father—my Carl Joe one—at all. Because he wasn't my real father. Don't you think they should have told me that a long time ago? Don't you think they should have let me find my real father?"

"Wait a minute. Let me get this straight. Your *father* is not your *father*? Did she tell you who your father is? Your *real* father?"

He said, "Yup."

"Wow. So who *is* it?"

"I can't tell."

"CARL RAY, YOU IMBECILE."

"What's the matter with *you*?"

"You can't make me promise and then not tell, and then tell, but only tell part. You just can't do that."

"But my mother would KILL me—"

"I don't care, Carl Ray. I don't care."

I thought we were going to have an accident, because right about then, the car in front put on its brake lights and I had to scream at Carl Ray and he jammed on the brakes and just missed that car by about six inches.

"So," I said, when we calmed down from almost being killed, "tell me who it is. Spit it out."

"I'm not saying a word," he said. "I promised my mother that I wouldn't tell anyone who it was until . . ."

"Until what?"

"Until I talk with someone."

"Who?" I said. "Is it your real father? Is that who? Is that who you have to talk to first?"

Carl Ray drove and drove and drove. And just before we pulled in our driveway, Carl Ray made me *promise* (again!!!) not to say anything to anyone under any circumstances. I said, "What about Alex? Not even to Alex?" and he said, "No!" so I promised, but I'm not sure I can keep that promise.

So we got HOME. Finally. Everybody was eating dinner and they were so surprised because they didn't expect us until Friday and they were hopping all around and talking all at once.

Dennis and Dougie were going on about some presents, Maggie was going on about Beth Ann calling all the time, Tommy was going on about a tractor, and Mom and Dad were going on about Mrs. Furtz.

The bit about the presents was this: During the week that we were gone, boxes started arriving—a lawn mower for Dad, a bicycle for Dougie, a kiddie tractor for Tommy, ice skates for Dennis, a coat for Maggie, and a coat for Mom. Then something for me.

"For me? Where *is* it?"

They said it was in my room. I went racing upstairs. There, in my room, was this rolltop desk with a million little cubbyholes for paper, pens, and all that stuff. I was never so surprised in my whole life.

Everybody knew it was Carl Ray. We were all hugging him and thanking him. Boy, did he look embarrassed.

How about that Carl Ray?

Next, the bit about Beth Ann: Maggie said that Beth Ann must have called thirty times, and Carl Ray better hurry up and call her before she explodes.

Everybody thought that was real funny—except Carl Ray, that is.

Mom said that on the day we left (last Friday), Mrs. Furtz came over. She was a basket case. She said that she had to see Carl Ray, but they explained that we had left. She wanted his phone number. They explained about the phone.

Mrs. Furtz said she had to talk to Carl Ray about the ring. Carl Ray gave me a sick look when they said this, but he said he would go over there tomorrow (which is today, but I'll tell about that later).

Boy, what an exciting evening. But most of all, it was so wonderful to be HOME. I know how Odysseus must have felt.

When things quieted down a little, I phoned Alex. I was dying to talk to him and surprise him, because he wasn't expecting me until tomorrow. But there was no answer. I called about ten times last night and ten times today. Where IS he? He was supposed to be home on Tuesday. I can't stand it. If I don't see him pretty soon, I'm going to burst. Calm down, Mary Lou. Maybe his family decided to stay longer in Michigan. Maybe they got in an accident. Oh, Lord. Calm down, Mary Lou.

I just tried phoning again. NO ANSWER. Oh, Alpha and Omega!

Calm down.

Beth Ann. I will talk about Beth Ann to get my mind off Alex. Carl Ray called her last night and went over to her house (after he put on a ton of Canoe). She called today, but Carl Ray was over at Mrs. Furtz's, only I didn't tell her that. I just said he was out. Then she went on and on for hours about how much she had missed him and how wonderful it is to have him back, only he seems tired and sad, she said, and on and on, and did he miss her, and what did he say, and on and on. I made a bunch of stuff up.

She didn't say one word about missing me. Friendship, boy.

She did say, however, that she went to the GGP pajama party and that it was "fine," but she "couldn't really say" what she did there. (She's starting to sound just like Carl Ray.)

"What do you mean, you can't really say? Don't you remember?"

"Oh," she said, "I remember. Only I can't *say*."

"Why not?" I asked.

Pause. Pause.

"Why *not*, Beth Ann?" She can be a real pain sometimes.

Pause. Pause. Pause.

I was about to hang up the stupid phone.

"Promise not to get mad?" she said.

ANOTHER ROTTEN STUPID PROMISE! I almost threw the phone out of the window.

Quite calmly, I said, "I promise not to get mad, Beth Ann."

Pause. "Well," she started, "I've been voted into GGP . . ."

I felt my teeth gnashing together.

". . . and, oh please don't be mad, Mary Lou, but I accepted their invitation to join, and I can't tell about the pajama party because it is supposed to be secret."

"What? A pajama party is secret?" Gnash. Gnash.

"Mary Lou, you promised not to get mad—"

"I am NOT mad," I said, and I hung up the stupid phone. Honestly.

I will change the subject. I will not waste any more paper on Beth Ann Bartels.

I showed Maggie the book that Sally Lynn gave me about sex and she seemed *extremely* interested in it. I let her borrow it. I've already looked through the good parts.

It's a little advanced, I think, for me. It's probably a little advanced even for my *parents*.

WHERE IS ALEXXX??? (I just phoned again: no answer. Groan.)

Mrs. Furtz. Tell about Mrs. Furtz. Okay.

Carl Ray looked really pathetic when he got back from seeing Mrs. Furtz today. He said she wanted to know where he got the ring.

I've been wondering about that myself. "So?" I said. "Where *did* you get it? And if you're going to ask me to promise not to tell, I am gonna blast you one."

"I told her that Mr. Furtz gave it to me before he went into the hospital that day."

"WHAT??? Are you saying *Mr. Furtz* gave you that ring? The one you turned around and gave back to *Mrs. Furtz*? Is that what you're saying here? Could you tell me exactly why it is that everybody's always giving you things, Carl Ray? Could you please tell me that? You hardly knew Mr. Furtz. You worked for him—what—a day? A lousy day? And he gives you a ring? Is that what you're trying to tell me?"

I would not make a very good detective. I would want to beat the information out of people. Which is what I felt like doing right then to Carl Ray. I am so impatient.

"Why, Carl Ray? Why did he give it to you?"

"Look, Mary Lou. I'll tell you all about it tomorrow,

okay? I have to go think awhile. I promise I'll tell you tomorrow."

Oh brother. He'd better tell me or I'm going to kill him.

Just phoned Alex again. No answer. Groannnn. I'm going to bed. Please let him be home tomorrow, Athene, please.

Saturday, August 4

Oh, King of Kings and Alpha and Omega! I am definitely going to go cra-zeeee.

First of all, that beefbrained Beth Ann. She called here four times this morning wanting to talk to Carl Ray. The first two times I said he was still in bed and I wasn't going to wake him up. The third time she begged and moaned, so I went up to wake him, and he wasn't there! So I told her that and she wanted to know where he was.

I said, "I'm not my brother's keeper, Beth Ann."

She said, "He's not your stupid brother, Mary Lou."

She called again an hour later and wanted to know if he was back yet. I said, "Nope." She wanted to know when he would be back.

I said, "I'm not my brother's k—"

Then Carl Ray came home. I told him about besotted

Beth Ann. He said he'd call her later. I said, "Good for you, Carl Ray." I was glad he didn't go rushing to the phone.

Then I asked him if he'd drive me to the drugstore. I didn't have to go to the drugstore, but I knew that was the only way I was going to get him alone so he could tell me the rest of the story about the ring.

I should mention, however, that before Carl Ray came home, I called Alex again. He wasn't home. I'm going to die.

So Carl Ray and I got in the car.

"Okay," I said, "finish your story, and don't give me any business about 'What story?' You know exactly what I mean. About Mrs. Furtz. She wanted to know where you got the stupid ring and you told her that Mr. Furtz gave it to you, and I asked why, and you didn't answer. And by the way, I want to know exactly why you came here to Easton and exactly who your father is. I want to know it all, Carl Ray."

He gave me one of those mournful looks. "I came here because my mother said that my father—the real one—lived here in Easton."

"In *Easton*? God! Easton?" I was trying to think of everybody I knew who was old enough to be Carl Ray's father. I had this horrible thought that what if it was *my* father? That was too horrible to even think about.

Then I thought of Mr. Furtz, but Mr. Furtz was dead and, besides, he didn't even know Carl Ray until Carl Ray got a job at the hardware store. Then I thought of Mr. Cheevey, for some reason, and as soon as I thought of Mr. Cheevey, I thought, *Of course!* Mr. Cheevey has those long arms and those long legs and that skinny body and that little bitty head and those freckles. Boy, have I been stupid! All that other stuff—the money and the college education—must have come from his real father. *Of course!* Mr. Cheevey has lots of money. But eck—Alex and Carl Ray as brothers? Eck. I said, "WHO IS IT? WHO IS YOUR FATHER?"

"You don't have to yell."

"I DO! I DO! I DO!" I stopped. I counted to twenty. I breathed deeply. "Okay, Carl Ray," I said, in this very sweet and soft voice. "Did you find your father here in Easton?"

He nodded.

Softly, sweetly, I said, "Who is it, Carl Ray?"

He looked all mournful. "I have to do one more thing first, and then I'll tell you."

Aargh. "And when might that be? I am only asking for an approximate time. Tomorrow? Wednesday? Next week? Next year? In ten years?"

"Pretty soon."

"Very good. Very good indeed, Carl Ray. Thank you

for telling me all of this." Sometimes when you talk with Carl Ray for a while, you begin to lose your marbles and talk like an idiot.

Sunday, August 5

Oh, King of Kings!

Alex is home! Finally! Sigh.

I haven't seen him yet. I called and called his house all day and was just about to expire from despair because no one was home, no answer, no nothing.

And then, after dinner, he called. They made a "side trip" to visit some old friend of his father's and that's why they didn't get back on Tuesday. He's fine, he missed me, and he wants me to go over there tomorrow. Maybe Carl Ray will drive me over. I don't think I can wait until tomorrow night. God, I'm hopeless.

Right after I finished talking to Alex, the phone rang and Maggie answered it, and she said it was for Carl Ray. He mainly listened, and every once in a while he would say, "Yup," and "Okay." I knew it wasn't Beth Ann, because when he's talking to her on the phone, he messes with his hair.

When he hung up, I said, "So, who was it?"

He said, "Just somebody. Nothin' important."

Honestly. People. I didn't even ask him about any of his secrets. I think the trick with Carl Ray is that you have to give him a little time. You have to be patient. I am going to learn to be more patient.

Monday, August 6

Oh, Deity, Omnipotent, Alpha and Omega, King of Kings and Supreme Being!!!!

You won't believe it.

You really won't.

But then again, maybe you will. Maybe you haven't been as stupid as I have been.

Calm down, Mary Lou. Tell it from the beginning.

First of all, while Carl Ray was at work today, the mail came and there was a letter for Carl Ray from Aunt Radene. I kept looking at that letter. I held it to the light but couldn't see anything at all. Then I examined the flap to see if it would open easily. Stuck down tighter than anything. I thought about trying to steam it open, but the last time I did that (with one of Maggie's letters) I burned my hand, and it didn't work anyway, and Maggie could tell someone had been trying to get her letter open and she went berserk.

So I had to wait.

As soon as Carl Ray got home, I gave him the letter. Then I stood there while he looked at it. He didn't open it. He started up to his room. I said, "It's from your mother."

He said, "I know."

God.

Then I asked him if he'd take me over to Alex's after dinner. He said, "Sure," and he went on upstairs.

He came down for dinner with a tie on! Everybody started teasing him.

"Goin' out with Beth Ann?" Dennis asked.

"Hot date, huh?" said Dougie.

"Didn't know you owned a tie, Carl Ray," Maggie said.

But Carl Ray just ate his dinner.

Then he drove me to Alex's. He seemed so *nervous*. I figured Aunt Radene must have really shaken him up by her letter. So I said, "What did your mom have to say?"

"Oh, stuff."

"Yeah. Stuff. Like what?" I get right to the point, don't I? So much for patience.

"She told me that I could tell people about my real father if I wanted to. She said she had a long talk with my other father—the Carl Joe one—and he understands now why I was so mad at first and why I had to come up here to find him—the other father. He—Carl Joe was jealous, she said."

I counted to ten. "So is it okay for you to tell who your real father is? Can you tell me now? Can you?" He pulled into the Big Boy parking lot and stopped the car. I counted to twenty. I breathed very deeply.

And then HE SAID IT. He just came right out and said, "Mr. Furtz is my father."

Holy cow. Alpha and Omega. All I could say was, *"Mr. Furtz?"*

And Carl Ray sat there nodding like an idiot, but all of a sudden he started to cry, and all of a sudden I remembered that Mr. Furtz was *dead*, and so I started patting Carl Ray on the shoulder. Mr. Furtz! When he calmed down a little, he told me the whole story. If I put it down just as Carl Ray said it, with me in between counting to thirty and forty and fifty and holding my breath, it would take me a whole journal. So I'll summarize it to the best of my ability.

Here goes: When Aunt Radene first told Carl Ray that Uncle Carl Joe was not his real father, Carl Ray was really mad. He thought she should have told him sooner. He made her tell him who it really was, and she said it was a man named Charlie Furtz.

Aunt Radene and Mr. Furtz had been dating for a year when they went to a New Year's Eve party in Easton. That's the party my parents talk about, where Uncle Carl Joe and Aunt Radene fell in love "at first sight." Aunt

Radene stopped dating Mr. Furtz and started seeing Uncle Carl Joe and right away they knew they were going to get married. Then Aunt Radene discovered she was pregnant and it was Mr. Furtz's baby. (Does this sound like a soap opera or what?) But Uncle Carl Joe said it didn't matter to him. So they got married right away and nobody ever knew that Carl Ray was anybody's baby but their very own.

Then, about six months ago, Aunt Radene read an article in a magazine that said you should always tell children if they were adopted, that they had a right to know. Uncle Carl Joe didn't think she should tell Carl Ray because he wasn't exactly adopted. Aunt Radene was his real mother, after all. And Uncle Carl Joe said, "What is a father anyway? Isn't it someone who raises a child as his own?" But Aunt Radene worried and worried and finally she told Carl Ray.

Are you following this?

Anyway, she could not have known Carl Ray would go all berserk on her, and that he would insist on knowing who his real father was and where he lived. As soon as Aunt Radene told him it was Charlie Furtz and he lived in Easton (at least she thought he still lived there), Carl Ray said he was going to go find him and no one could stop him. Uncle Carl Joe got mad. That's when Aunt Radene wrote to my parents asking if Carl Ray could come up here and stay with us awhile.

"God!" I said. "Did you know Mr. Furtz lived right across the street from us?"

Carl Ray said no. He had looked in the phone book under Furtz and there was one Charles Furtz, who lived on the other side of Easton. Carl Ray went to that address, but the lady living there said the Furtzes had moved to a bigger house. She wasn't sure where this bigger house was. He was all depressed, but that very night he came outside when Dennis and I were sitting on the curb, and he heard us say the name Furtz and he couldn't believe it. He decided it was fate.

The next day he went to the hardware store and he told Mr. Furtz who he was, and that he was Mr. Furtz's son.

"God!" I said. "What'd he say? Was he mad? Did he believe you? God!"

"He just looked at me a long time and asked me when my birthday was and he thought awhile and said that well, I did look like him a little bit. He wanted to call my mother, but when I said she didn't have a phone, he said he would write to her. Then he offered me a job—and on the first day of work, he gave me the ring."

"It *was* Mr. Furtz's ring?" That's when I realized that Mr. Furtz (Charlie), Uncle Carl Joe, and Carl Ray all have the same initials: C.F.

Carl Ray nodded. "I didn't know this then, but my mother had given him that ring a long time ago. That day he went to the doctor, and then to the hospital, and a few days later . . ." Carl Ray started crying again.

It was awful. I was crying too.

Later, Carl Ray said that he only just learned from Mr. Biggers that when Mr. Furtz heard that he had to go into the hospital, he was afraid that he was going to die. He had a premonition. So he contacted Mr. Biggers.

"The money! The college education! That was from Mr. Furtz?"

Boy, have I been stupid. I should have guessed this a long time ago. I've been so wrapped up in Alex Cheevey that I didn't see anything right in front of my nose.

Carl Ray said that yes, it was all from Mr. Furtz, although Mr. Biggers didn't tell him that at the time. Carl Ray didn't know that for sure until he went home and told Aunt Radene everything. She was very upset about Mr. Furtz dying. She wished Carl Ray had told her that sooner. He felt real bad about that, I could tell. But Aunt Radene said that would explain the letter she got from Mr. Furtz, saying he wanted to leave something for Carl Ray, and she had written back saying only "You don't have to." But apparently Mr. Furtz didn't get that letter. He was dead already. Mrs. Furtz got it and she didn't understand it.

When we got back from West Virginia, Carl Ray went to Mr. Biggers again, and he said he needed to know if it was Mr. Furtz who gave him the money, and Mr. Biggers said he would have to check if he could divulge the name. That's who called Carl Ray on Sunday. Mr. Biggers. And he said, yes, it was Mr. Furtz who had left Carl Ray the money and all.

How am I doing? Like I said, this took Carl Ray hours to spit out.

Sometime in there I asked Carl Ray if he had told Mrs. Furtz any of this, and he said that yes, he told her today.

"Well, God," I said. "Was she mad? I bet she was really mad. Wasn't she? She didn't even know that you were Mr. Furtz's son?"

He said, "Nope. She didn't know. But I think she was a little relieved."

"Relieved?"

"She said odd things had been happening. First, right after Mr. Furtz died, a letter arrived for him that said, 'Dear Charlie, You don't have to. Sincerely, Radene.' Mrs. Furtz thought he had been seeing some other woman. Then I gave her the ring, and she knew it was Mr. Furtz's. He had always kept it in this little box on his dresser, and he told her it was from an old girlfriend. He never wore it. She couldn't figure out how I got it. She thought I *stole* it. Can you imagine that?"

"Didn't she want to know why Mr. Furtz never told her about you?"

"When I told her that Mr. Furtz only just found out himself—that I was his son—right before he went in the hospital, she said that she knew he would have told her soon enough. And when I got ready to leave, she said, 'I'm just glad to know that there's a little more of Charlie left in the world now that he's gone.' "

Can you imagine that? It made *me* cry.

So. We sat there a long time. I felt real bad for Carl Ray. Why did Mr. Furtz have to die right after Carl Ray found him? Finally, Carl Ray started the car again, and when we pulled into Alex's driveway, I asked him where he was going, all dressed up. Carl Ray said, "To the cemetery. I want to talk to my—uh, my father."

Well, I started bawling like mad, and Carl Ray had to pat *me* on the shoulder. Then I asked him if he wanted me to come with him, but he said, "Nope."

When Alex answered the door, he just stood there. He looked at me as if he'd never seen me before.

I thought I was going to die. Oh boy, I thought. He doesn't like me anymore. Then I thought, I look terrible from all this crying and he's thinking I'm uglier than he remembered. Then I thought, He's going to tell me it's all over. We're finished.

He seemed so *nervous*. I thought, Sure, he *ought* to be nervous. He's going to tell me it's all over and maybe he thinks I'll punch him or something.

"Come on in," he said.

On the antique side of the room was Mrs. Cheevey, and on the modern side was Mr. Cheevey. When they saw us, they jumped up.

"So who's going to start?" Mrs. Cheevey said.

We looked at her. Start what?

Then Mrs. Cheevey said, "Okay, okay, okay. Let's start with Mary Kay. Oooh! A rhyme: *Okay*, Mary *Kay*. Ha, ha, ha."

"It's Mary *Lou*," Alex said.

Then, all of a sudden, I started talking. I was so upset about Carl Ray, I had to tell someone. So I told them all about Carl Ray and Mr. Furtz. I went on and on and on. I told them everything. They kept saying, "Poor Carl Ray," and "How astonishing," and "Poor Mr. Furtz," and on and on.

And after I finished babbling away like an idiot, I felt better.

Then Alex said, "Want to go see my fishing lures?"

The funny thing is Alex really *does* have a collection of fishing lures. We went out into the garage to look at them, and then it happened. The Big Event.

He KISSED me!!!!

Sighhhhhhh.

Right there, in the garage, beside the fishing lures. He just leaned over and kissed me. It was simple as anything. Still, I was glad I had practiced. And you know what? It didn't taste a *bit* like chicken.

Sighhhh.

After the kiss, we looked at some more fishing lures. It was a little embarrassing, if you want to know the truth. I am sure we were both thinking, Wow! We did it! We kissed. Wow! And there we were saying things like, "Oh that's a nice lure," and "Here's my favorite," and all that sum and substance. Then, right before we went back into the house, we kissed one more time. I started that one. I figured maybe it was my turn. Is that how it goes?

Sighhhhh.

Finally Mr. Cheevey took me home, and right after I got home, Carl Ray returned and told everybody at my house his whole, long, sad, complicated story.

I thought they were going to keel over at least a dozen times. Carl Ray didn't cry again, but everybody kept telling him how sorry they were about Mr. Furtz. It was as if Mr. Furtz had just that very day died all over again. While I was sitting there listening to Carl Ray, I kept looking at my parents and I decided I was going to pay more attention to them from now on. I really am. You know what Carl Ray said? He said, "I'm lucky, actually. I still have a real father." And we all knew exactly what he meant. Uncle Carl Joe *is* his real father because, as he says, a father is someone who raises you and takes care of you.

I kept thinking about this time when I was much younger. I was lying in bed one night, feeling really sick. I must have been moaning or something, because my dad came in the room. I told him my stomach was going crazy. He asked me if I was going to throw up, and when I said, "Maybe," he said I should sit up. And then, before I could even get to the bathroom, I started throwing up, and do you know what he did? He put his hands out to catch it. I threw up right into his hands. And I remember thinking, even though I was only about seven years old at the time, Wow, only a mother or father would do *that.*

And I'm sure Uncle Carl Joe has done lots of things like that for Carl Ray.

Tuesday, August 7

I still can hardly believe yesterday. When I woke up this morning, I had to go back and read last night's journal entry to be sure I hadn't imagined all of it.

King of Kings!

I sure had weird dreams last night. In my dreams, everybody kept getting all mixed up and running together.

My father turned into Uncle Carl Joe who turned into Mr. Furtz who turned into Mr. Cheevey. Mrs. Cheevey turned into Mrs. Furtz who turned into Aunt Radene.

Beth Ann called here a million times today while Carl Ray was at work. She wanted to know where in the world Carl Ray was last night, and she wanted to know how long he was gone and why he didn't come over to her house and on and on and on. I didn't tell her any of the *news*; I figure Carl Ray will do that soon enough. I just said I wasn't my cousin's keeper. That made her mad.

I couldn't see Alex today (groannnn), but I'll see him tomorrow.

Sighhhh.

Wednesday, August 8

Saw Alex tonight!!! Brain is complete mush as a result!!!

Two more kisses.

I LOVE ALEX CHEEVEY!!!

Thursday, August 9

Alpha and Omega, school starts again in three weeks! How did that happen??? Where has summer gone???

Saw Alex again tonight. Two kisses. Sighhhhhh.

Friday, August 10

Couldn't see Alex today, but he invited me to a picnic with his parents on Sunday. He invited Carl Ray too, but Carl Ray got a letter from his other father, Uncle Carl Joe, and Uncle Carl Joe wants him to go home this weekend. He wants to talk to him.

I refused one hundred percent to go along with Carl Ray this time. Dennis is going to go. Poor thing. And I am not going to warn him about snappers or Booger Hill or the outhouse. He wouldn't believe me anyway, and he might as well find out the hard way.

Beth Ann is a basket case. Carl Ray told her on Tuesday night about Mr. Furtz being his father and all, and Beth Ann called me on Wednesday to ask if it was true. She doesn't think it's neat *at all.* She thinks it's sort of disgusting, and she told Carl Ray that. So Carl Ray didn't see her on Wednesday or Thursday.

So then Beth Ann called me about a million times on Wednesday and Thursday to ask why Carl Ray hadn't called her. Honestly. When I told her that Carl Ray was going to West Virginia this weekend, she started sniffling. How could he *do* that? How *could* he? And on and on.

Then she told me that she was going to another GGP pajama party on Saturday. I pretended I didn't hear.

Then she told me she had seen Derek-the-Di-viiiiine. Remember him? Her old gorgeous boyfriend? She saw him at the A&P. He was with a "tacky" girl in a "tacky" pink sweater and a "tacky" pair of slacks.

I had this terrible feeling that Beth Ann is the kind who would drop Carl Ray in a minute and go back to Derek-the-Di-viiiiine. She'd better not, that's all I can say.

Saturday, August 11

Oh, dreary day. Raining and pouring outside. Carl Ray and Dennis are gone. Mom made me go through all my old school clothes so she could figure out what I would need for, ugh, school in September.

I finished the *Odyssey* today. Sort of a strange ending.

Sacking the Suitors

Of course, Odysseus sacks all the suitors and hangs the maids who didn't conduct themselves very well in his absence. Odysseus's dog recognizes him before his wife does (honestly!). In fact, Penelope is going to make him sleep by himself until he goes on and on about their bed that he made with his own two hands and all. He goes into every single detail about how he made it, and finally Penelope believes that he is really Odysseus, her husband, and she goes all soppy over him.

Then, just when you think everything's happy and peachy again, a bunch of the suitors' relatives come to battle with Odysseus. More bloody battles, until Athene swoops down and says, basically, "Quit fighting or Zeus is going to be mad," and so they stop and that's the end.

I was sort of sorry it was over, to tell you the truth. No more rosy-fingered Dawn and swooping Athene and one-eyed monsters and disguises and revelations. Sigh.

I've started calling Alex "Poseidon (King of the Sea)," because of his fishing lures and all. The only thing is, ole Poseidon doesn't have a girlfriend (like Antony and Cleopatra, etc.), so Alex was having trouble trying to think up a nickname for me. I told him I wouldn't mind being called "Athene," because, after all, she is a goddess. Heh.

Sunday, August 12

My brain is three hundred percent mush—partly from being with Alex and partly from being with the Cheeveys all day. I'll tell about it tomorrow.

Monday, August 13

So. I'll start with yesterday. Lordie, Lordie.

We all went to Windy Rock. Alex and I took a long walk and climbed up to the actual Windy Rock. We found a place in the grass, and it was so nice there just sitting in the grass, with this little wind blowing all around us and the sky real clear and the sun warm on our arms and legs.

Sighhhhh.

So, let's see. Carl Ray and Dennis got back from their trip. You should have heard Dennis talking about it. He liked the outhouse just about as much as I did, and while he was there, he went swimming in the swimming hole and Lee Bob scared him talking about the "snapper," and sure enough, John Roy took Dennis up Booger Hill, and sure enough, John Roy took him all the way up to the cabin, and sure enough, when they got there John

Roy started screaming, "Convict!" and took off and Dennis got lost. Dennis also said that Carl Ray drove like a maniac and they were lucky to get home alive. Does all of this sound familiar?

I asked Carl Ray about his father (the Uncle Carl Joe one). He said everything was much, much better. Carl Ray told Uncle Carl Joe what he had told us about being lucky that he still had a real father. And Uncle Carl Joe said he was happy to hear that and he would always be there when Carl Ray needed him.

Then Carl Ray wanted to know if Beth Ann had called, so I told him all about her eight million calls. Carl Ray went to the cemetery again last night, and he must have come home very late, because I didn't even hear him come in.

At dinner tonight, Carl Ray casually mentioned that Mrs. Furtz had asked him if he would like to live with them.

DAD: What???

MOM: What???

MAGGIE: What???

DENNIS: What'd he say? I missed it! What'd you say, Carl Ray?

ME: Mrs. Furtz wants to know if you'll go live with them? With the Furtzes?

DENNIS: What??? Is that what he said?

ME: Well, you're not going to do that, are you, Carl Ray?

DOUGIE: You're going to leave?

TOMMY: NO! NOT LEAVING! *(Starts crying like mad.)*

DAD: Why don't you all just give Carl Ray a chance to answer?

MOM: Now that's a good idea.

ME: *(to Carl Ray)* Well?

DENNIS: Well?

DOUGIE: Well?

CARL RAY: I told her I'd have to think about it. She said she'd like to have a man around the house, and I could kill spiders and help out and get to know my sort-of-brothers and my sort-of-sister.

DAD: Oh.

MOM: Oh.

TOMMY: NOT LEAVING! NOT LEAVING!

Now, you know what? A month ago, if someone had asked Carl Ray to leave our house and go live elsewhere, I would have jumped up and down for joy; I would have turned cartwheels; I would have been as happy as a clam in seaweed. But the funny thing is when Carl Ray said that about Mrs. Furtz asking him to go live there, I was mad at her. Who does she think she is, all of a sudden deciding to take Carl Ray like that? And what about Uncle Carl Joe? How would Mrs. Furtz feel if somebody decided to just up and take Cathy or Barry or little David away?

People just don't think sometimes.

Tuesday, August 14

1) I didn't see Alex. He had to work all day.
2) Carl Ray broke up with Beth Ann!
3) I found out what GGP means: Girls Going Places. Imagine. How dumb.

Wednesday, August 15

Christy called me today and asked me if I'd like to come to a GGP pajama party on Saturday night. She said it was only for members and a few girls who were "under consideration." I said I was busy. I don't think I would have said that two months ago, but something has happened to me this summer.

I didn't see Alex today because he and his father went fishing after work.

Thursday, August 16

I LOVE ALEX CHEEVEY!!! He sent me a red rose with a card that said, "To Athene, from Poseidon."

I think I am losing my brains.

Carl Ray still hasn't decided about moving in with the Furtzes.

Friday, August 17

Went to the movies with Alex. That's what I call heaven.

Sighhhhhh.

Saturday, August 18

Beth Ann went to the GGP pajama party. Big deal.

Sunday, August 19

Carl Ray told Mrs. Furtz today that he wasn't going to move in with them!

Beth Ann called to tell me that Derek-the-Di-viiiiine came over to her house after dinner. She also said to be sure and tell Carl Ray. I didn't.

Monday, August 20

Oh, nooooooo.

I'm dyyyyying.

Alex and I broke up (I think).

It happened like this (groannnn): We went to the park after dinner. Then we walked home to my house. Then he said good-bye. What? No kiss? He started walking away.

That's why I think we broke up.

I'm dyyyyying.

Tuesday, August 21

No word from Alex. I am truly dying. I can't breathe.

And stupid ole Beth Ann wormed her way back into

Carl Ray's heart. They're back together. Lucky them. I'm *reallllll* happy. I really am.

Wednesday, August 22

Christy called today to say I had only one more chance to come to a GGP pajama party. I said, "Very big deal." She got mad and hung up.

I'm becoming a rotten person.

Thursday, August 23

Today the florist delivered another rose from Poseidon!

When I got the rose and the card, I tried to call Alex, but his mother said he was at work. So I said, "Please tell him that Athene called."

She said, "I thought this was Mary Lou."

"It is," I said.

"Oh. So I'll tell Alex you called."

"Well, no. Could you tell him that *Athene* called?"

"Isn't this Mary Lou?"

Groannnnnnn.

Alex called when he got home. He said, "My mother said that you called but that you were all mixed up and didn't even know your own name."

Huh.

I thanked him for the rose and the card. Then I took a deep breath and asked him why he didn't kiss me the other night. And do you know what he said? He said he forgot! He *forgot*?

Boys.

Friday, August 24

Well. What a strange evening.

I don't exactly know how this happened, but Alex and I went out with Beth Ann and Carl Ray tonight. We went to play miniature golf.

It was a three-kiss evening. Sighhhhhh.

Carl Ray said, when he and I got home, "You're okay, Mary Lou."

Hmmm.

I can't seem to write any more. Muse? Where have you gone?

Saturday, August 25

Today Alex and I sorted out his fishing lures and cleaned

their garage. That won't sound very interesting to you, but you've never seen their garage! It's filled with all kinds of amazing stuff: old wooden skis, pogo sticks, a five-foot-high stuffed bear, a cardboard igloo, two mannequins (man and woman), a box of wigs, a fake palm tree, a parachute, a framed picture of a groundhog, a collection of mounted eels, a tuba, and on and on and on.

We called Carl Ray from Alex's house to see if he and Beth Ann wanted to go out again, but Carl Ray said he had to talk to Beth Ann about something, and he thought he'd better do it alone!

Alex and I tried to guess what that was all about. We had two ideas: Maybe Carl Ray is going to ask her to marry him (unlikely), or maybe Carl Ray is going to break up with her (why?).

Carl Ray still isn't home, so I don't know yet what that was all about. I left a note on his dresser that said, "Carl Ray, you're okay. P.S. It's a *rhyme*! From M.L."

Sunday, August 26

The worst, worst, worst thing has happened.

Carl Ray is in the hospital.

We got the call at three this morning. He had been at Beth Ann's, then he went to the cemetery, and then he was driving home and ran off the road and into a ditch and his car flipped right over.

You know what I thought when we got the call? I thought, "Snapper!" It scares me half to death, that something can happen just like that.

Carl Ray is unconscious. He has two broken legs, one broken arm and some broken ribs.

We spent all day at the hospital. The nurses only let Mom and Dad in the room. It's real bad. Dad sent a telegram to Aunt Radene. I don't feel much like writing.

I hope Carl Ray is going to be all right.

Monday, August 27

Please, gods, let Carl Ray be all right. He's still unconscious. Please don't let his time be up.

Tuesday, August 28

Aunt Radene, Uncle Carl Joe, all their kids, Mrs. Furtz and her kids, and all of us were at the hospital today. Everyone is praying like mad for Carl Ray to wake up.

I got to go in for five minutes today and see him. He looks so pitiful, lying there all pale and bruised and his plastered-up legs and arm sticking out and these tubes jabbed into him. I talked to him as if he could hear me. I said, "Carl Ray, you just have to wake up, because all these people *need* you to wake up. I have a feeling, Carl Ray, that a lot of these people still have some things to say to you." And then I told him what I had to say. I apologized for every rotten thing I ever did to him or said about him. I told him he was pretty okay.

Then, when I was back in the waiting room, I kept thinking of the way Carl Ray grins sometimes, and all those presents Carl Ray bought everyone, and Carl Ray saying, "Mary Lou, you're okay," and I kept thinking about that note I left on his dresser that he never even saw.

Wednesday, August 29

Carl Ray is not okay. He won't wake up, and the doctors told Aunt Radene and Uncle Carl Joe today that he might not *ever* wake up. How can such a thing like this happen?

I can't write about it.

Thursday, August 30

Uncle Carl Joe sits by Carl Ray's bed all day and all night.

He won't leave. Mrs. Furtz invited Aunt Radene and all my cousins to stay at their house because we don't have much room. In a way, I'm glad that Mr. Furtz isn't alive to see what has happened to Carl Ray.

I read back over all these journals today. All those awful things I said about Carl Ray. I only hope that Carl Ray knows that I didn't mean them and that it wasn't his fault that I was being so insensitive. I was only starting to see all the good things about him when this happened. Most of those things that used to make me mad about Carl Ray (the way he didn't ever talk and the way he snuck up on you and how much he ate and the way he didn't make his bed) are the things that I most like to remember now—not just the good things, like the way he held Tommy's hand that day at the funeral parlor and how he told Tommy all about God coming to get Mr. Furtz's soul, and always driving me places, and never saying a mean word about anyone, and bringing me back home from West Virginia early just because I was homesick, and on and on.

Those other things that used to drive me crazy are just part of Carl Ray, and once you get used to him, you wouldn't expect him to be any different. Suppose he *did* make up his bed and suppose he clomped around so you could hear him coming and suppose he ate like a bird and suppose he talked on and on like Beth Ann? Would those things be very important? Do they really matter? Remember Carl Ray acting like a monster, running around making funny noises? And can't you hear Carl Ray saying, "Don't rightly know"? Does anyone else say that? Isn't it just like Carl Ray?

Friday, August 31

Carl Ray is still unconscious.

I read back through the journals *again*. When I was writing them, I thought I noticed everything. I was keeping a record. But I didn't notice diddly-squat. I didn't even notice anything about Carl Ray being homesick or Carl Ray and Mr. Furtz, or how he felt after Mr. Furtz died. How could a person like me go along and go along, feeling just the same from day to day, and then all of a sudden look back and see that I didn't *see* much of anything? And that I've been changing all along? I don't even recognize myself when I read back over these pages.

Once my father told me that bad things happen sometimes to remind us we are mortal and to remind us to appreciate people more. We're not like Zeus or Athene, who can live forever and help people out of trouble.

I told Alex today that the awful thing about starting to like people was that if something happens to them, there is nothing you can do to make everything like it was before, and all the time you keep thinking of the things you wish you had said or done.

Alex said, "So does that mean you shouldn't like people?"

And even though I didn't know I thought this, I said, "Well, of course not! That's just the way it is. If you didn't let yourself *like* people, you'd shrivel up."

"Exactly," he said. "Exactly." One kiss.

Aunt Radene says that you just have to do your best to make the world a better place. I said I wasn't so sure I could make the world a better place, and she said, "Oh, you already have, Mary Lou, you already have."

How does a person ever know that for sure?

Saturday, September 1

Beth Ann told me today that when Carl Ray came to see her that night, before he had the accident, he told her that he was moving back to West Virginia. And then he went to see Mr. Furtz in the cemetery. Beth Ann was all upset because she had had a big fight with Carl Ray when he said he was moving. Now she wishes she could take back everything she said. I told her that I was sure Carl Ray knew she didn't mean it, that she only said those things because she would miss him.

Alex visited Carl Ray in the hospital today, and he took Carl Ray a fishing lure. He told Carl Ray (even though Carl Ray is still unconscious and couldn't hear him) that he would take him fishing when he woke up.

Sunday, September 2

Carl Ray must like fishing, because he woke up today! You've never seen a happier bunch of people in your life than Aunt Radene and Uncle Carl Joe and all my cousins, and my whole family, and the Furtzes and Alex and Beth Ann and all the nurses who have been taking care of Carl Ray.

You know what Carl Ray said when his father asked him how he was feeling? He said, "Don't rightly know." Uncle Carl Joe said that that was the most beautiful thing he had ever heard.

Athene has just swooped down and anointed Carl Ray and saved him from being thrashed around in the sea. What a relief!

What a terrific day!

Monday, September 3

Carl Ray is smiling all over the place now, getting better every minute. Uncle Carl Joe still sits by his bed all day long, watching Carl Ray and talking to him.

I was allowed to visit Carl Ray for five minutes today, and I gave him the note that I had put on his dresser, the one about him being okay. He pointed to the bedpan and said, "Do you think I could borrow your socks for the pee pot?" Carl Ray's getting a sense of humor. His wheel of fortune is spinning around to the top again.

I received a letter from school today with a list of my courses for next year—ack, next *week*! My English teacher is Mr. Birkway. He must be new, because I've never heard of him. So a complete stranger is going to read this journal and know all about our odyssey. Let's hope he is understanding and doesn't put red marks all over everything.

Tuesday, September 4

Carl Ray's better every day. He's coming home next week, and we've been busy decorating his room with signs. Aunt Radene and Uncle Carl Joe and all my cousins are going back to West Virginia today, although you can tell they don't really want to leave without Carl Ray, but he can't travel yet. When he's ready, Dad will take him back to West Virginia.

Carl Ray is hobbling all around the hospital already. He asks all the nurses to sign his casts. I think he's becoming more outgoing. Who would have imagined? That Carl Ray is full of surprises.

I decided to end this journal tomorrow. I only have a couple of pages left in this little blue book anyway (this is the sixth blue book I've used this summer). I asked Beth Ann and Alex if they did their journals. Alex said he only started his when he went to Michigan (I wonder if he wrote anything about me in it???), and Beth Ann said she thought she'd start it *today*! I know I wrote too much, but maybe I won't turn it in anyway. I'm not sure I want a total stranger to read this.

Wednesday, September 5

Our family went to Windy Rock today with the Cheeveys and the Furtzes and Beth Ann. What a day. We were all feeling sorry that Carl Ray was still in the hospital and wasn't able to come too, but Mrs. Cheevey said we would call it Carl Ray Day ("Ooh, a rhyme!") and she would take pictures and show them to Carl Ray, and when he gets out of the hospital, we could all go again.

I'm sure by now you can imagine all these people clumped together at Windy Rock and you can imagine Mrs. Cheevey darting all around and Beth Ann talking her head off and my brothers climbing trees and me and Alex sneaking off for one little kiss (well, heck!). So I don't have to write all that down.

I just want to say one more time that Carl Ray is okay!

I was trying to remember how Homer finished off the *Odyssey*, so I just read the ending again. It's a little corny, with Athene telling everyone to make peace, but I can't think of a better ending.

Sigh.

Summer's over.

Alpha and Omega!!

Read an excerpt from Sharon Creech's novel

The Great Unexpected

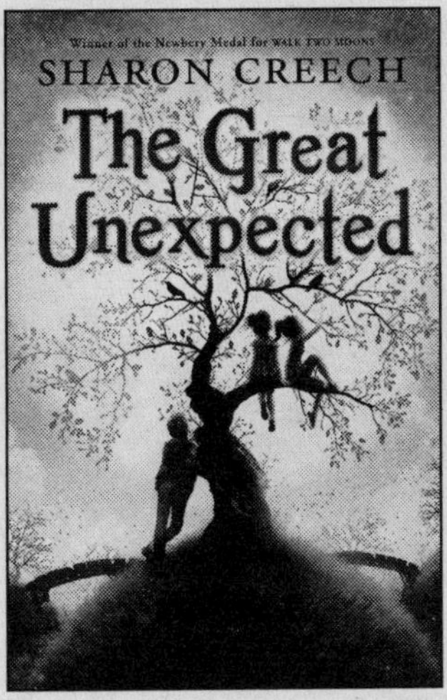

Prologue

My name is Naomi Deane and I grew up in Blackbird Tree, in the home of my guardians, Joe and Nula. Among the tales that Joe often told was that of a poor man who, while gambling, lost his house but won a donkey.

"A donkey?" the poor man wailed. "What do I want with a donkey? I cannot even feed a donkey."

"No matter," replied the donkey. "Reach into my left ear."

The poor man, though shocked that the donkey could talk, nonetheless reached into the donkey's ear and pulled out a sack of feed.

"Well, now," the poor man said. "That's a mighty handy ear. I wish it had food for *me* as well."

"Reach into my right ear," the donkey said.

And so the poor man reached into the donkey's right ear and pulled out a loaf of bread, a pot of butter, and a meat pie.

Joe went on like this, spinning out the tale, with the poor man pulling all sorts of things out of the donkey's ears: a stool, a pillow, a blanket, and, finally, a sack of gold.

I loved this story, but I always listened uneasily, fearing that something bad would be pulled from the donkey's ears. Even after I'd heard the tale many times, always the same, I still worried that the poor man might reach in and pull out a snapping turtle or an alligator or something equally unpleasant and unexpected.

Sensing my fear, Joe would say, "It's only a story, Naomi, only a story." He suggested that I say to myself, "I'm not in the story, I'm not in the story"—a refrain I could repeat so that I would feel less anxious.

And so each time the poor man would reach into the donkey's ears, I would tell myself, *I'm not in the story, I'm not in the story*, but it didn't help because a story was only interesting if I *was* in the story.

CHAPTER I

A Body Falls from a Tree

If you have never had a body fall out of a tree and knock you over, let me tell you what a surprising thing that is. I have had nuts fall out of a tree and conk my head. Leaves have fallen on me, and twigs, and a branch during a storm. Bird slop, of course, everyone gets that. But a body? That is not your usual thing dropping out of a tree.

It was a boy, close about my age, maybe twelve. Shaggy hair the color of dry dirt. Brown pants. Blue T-shirt. Bare feet. Dead.

Didn't recognize him. My first thought was, *Is this my fault? I bet this is my fault.* Nula once said I had a knack for being around when trouble happened. She had not been around other kids much, though, and maybe did not know that *most* kids had a knack for being around when trouble happened.

All I really wanted to do that hot day was go on down to the creek and hunt for clay in the cool, cool water. I was wondering if maybe I could deal with the body later, when the body said, "Am I dead?"

I looked at the body's head. Its eyes were closed.

"If you can talk, I guess you're not dead."

The body said, "When I open my eyes, how will I know if I'm dead or alive?"

"Well, now, you'll see me, you'll see the meadow, you'll see the tree you fell out of, so I guess you'll know you're alive."

"But how will I know if I'm here or if I'm at Rooks Orchard?"

"I don't know anything about any rook or any orchard, so I can pretty much guarantee that you are here and not there. Why don't you open your eyes and have a look around?"

And so the body opened his eyes and slowly sat up and looked all around—at the green meadow, at the cows in the distance, at the tree out of which he had fallen, and at me, and then he yelled, "Oh *no*!" and fell back on the ground and his eyes closed and he was dead again.

CHAPTER 2

Lizzie

No sooner had the body laid back down than I heard the warbling voice of Lizzie Scatterding. Lizzie often felt it necessary to sing—in a high, trembly, warbly opera voice—when she was outdoors.

"Oh, lar-de-dar, the sky so blue"—definitely Lizzie—"the fields so green, oh lar-de-dar—"

Lizzie was my friend, and usually I was glad to see her, but I was not sure how she was going to handle seeing the body at my feet. Sometimes Lizzie could be a little dramatic.

"Oh, lar-de-dar—Naomi! Is that you?" Lizzie stopped in the middle of the path and crossed her hands over her chest as if to keep her fragile heart steady. "Naomi!" She ran toward me, her frizzy mane flopping here and there.

"Ack! Naomi, what is *that*? Is that a person?" She inched her way around to stand in back of me so that I was her shield. "Who is it? Where'd it come from? Is it *dead*?" She clutched my shoulders. "You didn't *kill* it, did you?"

"It fell out of this here tree. I thought it was dead, but then it spoke, and now it's gone off again."

I kneeled beside the body and put my hand on its chest.

"Is it breathing?" Lizzie asked. "Take its pulse."

I held the body's wrist. "I can feel something gurgling in there."

"Oh, my! Then it's alive. Have you ever seen it before? What did it say when it spoke—before it went off again?"

"Something about a rook's orchard, or maybe a crook's orchard."

Lizzie's foot nudged the body's foot. "Maybe it was in an orchard place and a crook tried to kill it and so he hid in this tree and then when you came along—"

"Maybe we should stop calling it an *it*."

Lizzie studied the body's face. "Never saw it before, did you?"

"Nope."

"Look in its pockets, Naomi. See if it has something with its name on it."

"I'm not looking in any boy's pockets, dead or alive. You look."

Just then the body grunted. Lizzie skittered sideways like a crab.

"Good gracious! I swear to bats! It's alive!" Her hands were protecting her fragile heart again. "Naomi, the poor *thing*. What if his internal organs are hurt? What if he is bleeding to death and we don't even know it? Naomi, you must get help."

The body spoke. "Am I here—?"

Lizzie squealed. "It has a voice!"

Its eyes were still closed. "Am I here—or am I there?"

I touched his hand. "You're here."

"How will I know that?"

"Well, ding it, you are *here*. If you weren't here, you wouldn't be hearing me, would you? You'd be somewhere else. But you're not somewhere else, *you are here*!"

"Naomi, you don't have to be so harsh. It's a poor body lying there maybe bleeding to death and it just wants to know if it is here."

"Fine. Then you take over, Doctor Lizzie."

"I *will*." Lizzie carefully placed herself beside the body, folding her legs daintily beneath her. "Now," she cooed in the softest of tones, "everything will be just fine. We need to find out who you are and if you are injured in your internal organs."

The body was silent.

Lizzie inched a little closer. “Boy, can you tell me your name?”

Silence.

“Boy, do you have family around here?”

Silence.

“Naomi, do you have a cool cloth?”

“No, Lizzie, I do not happen to have a cool cloth on my person.”

“I feel we should put a cool cloth on this poor injured boy’s forehead.”

“I don’t have a cool cloth.”

Lizzie sighed a deep, meaningful sigh. “Oh, dear, oh, dear.” She lightly touched her fingers to the boy’s head. Then she leaned closer and blew on his forehead.

“Whatever are you doing, Lizzie?”

“I am cooling the poor boy, Naomi. I am bringing comfort until such time as he can rouse himself.”

“What if he can’t ever rouse himself? What if he dies for good?”

Lizzie tapped the boy’s shoulder. “Please do try your best to rouse yourself and tell us your name.”

Silence.

“I am pleading with you, boy.”

Silence.

“Naomi, you will have to get help. I will stay here with the poor, injured boy. Please go. Please hurry.”

But before I could move, the boy spoke again. "Don't take the gold."

"Naomi, he spoke! He told us not to take the gold!"

"I've got ears, Lizzie. I heard him." I tapped his arm. "What gold?"

Silence.

I scanned the area. No gold in sight. I asked louder: "WHAT GOLD?"

"Naomi, please don't shout at the poor, injured boy."

The boy opened his eyes.

"Naomi, he opened his eyes."

"For heaven's sake, Lizzie, I'm not blind."

"My name is Finn."

"Naomi, he said his name! He said his name! His name is Finn!"

"There isn't any gold," he said.

"Naomi, he said—"

"I know, I know what he said. There isn't any gold. There isn't any silver, either. There aren't any emeralds or rubies or diamonds—"

"—He didn't say any of that, Naomi. He only said about the gold."

"No gold," the boy repeated.

"See?" Lizzie said. "No gold."

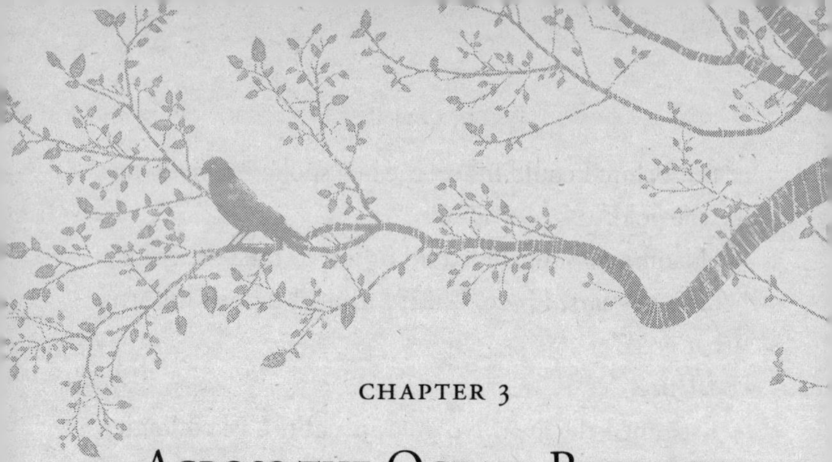

CHAPTER 3

Across the Ocean: Revenge

Mrs. Kavanagh

While Naomi and Lizzie were learning the name of the body that fell from a tree, across the ocean in a stately manor on the southeastern coast of Ireland, the elderly Mrs. Kavanagh paused as she wrote on a piece of fine parchment. She placed the pen to one side and tapped a finger on the desk.

"There. Enough for now." She smiled a wistful smile. "'T'will be a fine, fine revenge."

Her companion, Miss Pilpenny, recapped the pen. "Yes, Sybil, a fine and clever revenge."

"Shall we have a murder tonight?"

"Indeed, Sybil. Splendid notion."

"And then perhaps a little jam and bread."

"Indeed. That plum jam from the Master's orchard?"

Old Mrs. Kavanagh laughed, a sudden girlish burst that was followed by prolonged wheezing.

Miss Pilpenny rubbed the old lady's back until the wheezing subsided. "There, there. You can rest now."

Read all of the classics by Newbery Medal winner

Sharon Creech!

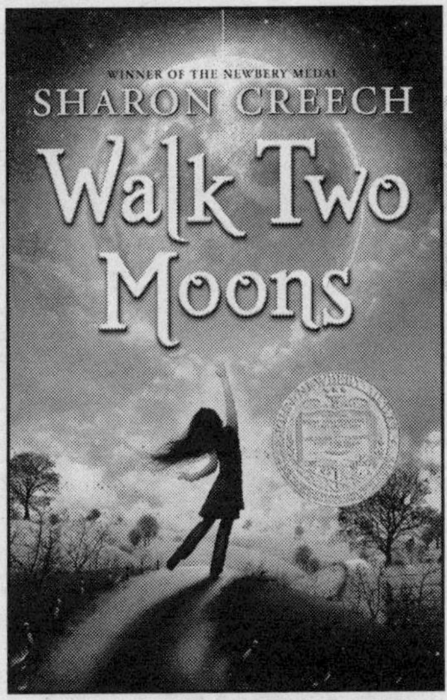

Newbery Medal Winner

Newbery Honor Book

www.sharoncreech.com

Joanna Cotler Books
An Imprint of HarperCollins*Publishers*

HARPER
An Imprint of HarperCollins*Publishers*

Read all of the classics by Newbery Medal winner

Sharon Creech!

- *Ruby Holler*—Carnegie Medal Winner
- *Absolutely Normal Chaos*
- *Pleasing the Ghost*
- *Chasing Redbird*
- *Bloomability*
- *Love That Dog*
- *Granny Torrelli Makes Soup*
- *Heartbeat*
- *Replay*
- *The Castle Corona*
- *Hate That Cat*
- *The Unfinished Angel*

www.sharoncreech.com

Joanna Cotler Books
An Imprint of HarperCollinsPublishers

HARPER
An Imprint of HarperCollinsPublishers